MONSTERS & MANUSCRIPTS

A LIBRARY WITCH MYSTERY

ELLE ADAMS

This book was written, produced and edited in the UK, where some spelling, grammar and word usage will vary from US English.

Copyright © 2021 Elle Adams
All rights reserved.

To be notified when Elle Adams's next book is released, sign up to her author newsletter.

1

"Time's up," said my Aunt Adelaide. "The exam is over."

I put down my pen, my wrist cramping, and laid it next to the stack of paper in front of me. My aunt flicked her wand and levitated the papers onto the desk at the front of the room before giving me a smile. "You can go, Rory."

Since I was the only person taking the exam, I didn't need to wait forever to be dismissed. The fact that my aunt was the examiner didn't hurt either. "Thanks, Aunt Adelaide."

I walked out of the examination room and into the lower floor of the library, releasing a shaky breath. *Done.* I'd successfully completed my latest magical theory exam, and I didn't think I'd done a terrible job either. I'd have to wait for the exams to be marked by an independent assessor from the local witch academy to find out my grade, but I hadn't run into any unpleasant surprises or trick questions. The fact that the exams were typically taken by preteens probably had something to do with that. Just one more reason I was glad the academy had agreed to let me take my exams in the privacy of the library rather than with a bunch of eight-year-olds.

As I skirted the cosy area at the back of the library known as the Reading Corner, a giant tawny owl loomed over me from the nearest bookshelf. "Finished another exam, did you?"

"Yeah, my magical theory test," I answered. "It covered hexes and spells, mostly."

"Oh, I recall that one," said Sylvester. "I hope you remembered to devote ample time to explaining the intricacies of enhancement hexes. They give bonus points if you can explain how to use a hex to switch your head around so that it faces backwards."

Sylvester's head rotated in demonstration, and I rolled my eyes at him. "You're just winding me up, Sylvester. That's not a thing."

"It is." His head rotated back around to face the front. "Your Aunt Candace tried it herself a few years ago and nearly got stuck like that."

"That sounds like her, but it definitely wasn't on the exam." I continued walking across the downstairs floor of the library, past students sitting at tables in groups. Most of the local academy students were preparing for their own exams, and so were the students from the town's sole university. I didn't blame them for hanging out here, considering the library was the best source of magical knowledge in the town, though I sometimes wished they'd take their spell practise sessions elsewhere.

Typically, Sylvester insisted on flying behind me all

the way through the Reference Section, offering a running commentary on the exam.

"Really, Sylvester." I halted before I reached the front desk. "The exam is Grade Three, not for PhD students. They're asking for basic hexes like turning one's hair green, not body modification."

Sylvester hooted in alarm. "You can't discuss the exam! It's forbidden!"

"That wasn't even a real example."

I was doubly glad that my aunt had refused to let Sylvester be the one to supervise my exam considering his ongoing habit of winding everyone up, especially me. While he might have *looked* like a typical owl familiar, he wasn't even an owl, but rather the animal-shaped embodiment of the library's entire store of knowledge. Of course, most people had no idea of his real identity, even Aunt Adelaide. I'd learned his secret by accident, and Sylvester had made it firmly clear that he'd appreciate it if I didn't tell anyone else. Grandma had known, I was sure, but she'd died before I'd ever had the chance to meet her.

I'd only moved to the library six months ago, and I hadn't even known the magical world existed before then. It'd been a serious adjustment to make, but as a self-certified bookworm, I'd taken to my family's library like a mermaid to water, and even Sylvester's oddities were just one more of the library's quirks. Even having to take exams after I'd thought I'd left school behind years ago was worth the trade-off.

I found my cousin Estelle behind the front desk helping a student check out a stack of textbooks almost as tall as he was. When he tottered away, she caught sight of me and beamed. "Rory, you survived!"

My brows shot up. "Should that be surprising? It's not like I had to wrestle a wild manticore."

"Watch Cass doesn't hear you saying that." She moved to open the front door for the student with the pile of books, and he staggered out into the town square.

Sylvester landed atop a nearby bookcase. "I can make some suggestions for your practical exam if you think it's too easy for you."

"Don't get any ideas." To Estelle, I added, "He's been banging on about this spell that can supposedly turn one's head around backwards and how it's the key to getting full marks on the exam. He also claimed that Aunt Candace tried it herself once."

"She did, but it's definitely not on the curriculum," said Estelle. "Really, Sylvester."

"I knew you were trying to worry me on purpose." I rolled my eyes at the owl. "Honestly. Where's Aunt Candace?"

"Upstairs working on her book, where else?"

"I figured she was trying to get out of exam supervision." Aunt Adelaide had had to work hard to persuade the local academy to let her supervise me while I sat the exams since they'd thought she might give me an unfair advantage. As she'd pointed out, though, there was little help she could give me that would make up for the disadvantage I'd started at by moving to the magical world as an adult, so they'd caved in. "It seems quiet in here, that's all."

Estelle shrugged. "It's exam season."

"Yes, it is," said Sylvester. "The students are slowly losing the will to live. Or maybe that's just in the Existential Crisis Division."

"Ha ha." I was a weirdo who *liked* studying, though I preferred writing essays in my own time rather than in the pressure of an examination room. "I don't expect Cass to be around, but it would have been nice if she or Aunt Candace had offered you a hand at running the desk while your mum was supervising me."

"I don't mind," Estelle said. "You're the one who had to sit an exam."

"It wasn't terrible." I rubbed my wrist. "I might have to brew a potion for wrist cramps, though. I haven't written that much in a long time."

Ironic given that our family's own magic worked by using words to conjure up whatever we needed, but it generally didn't involve writing essays, and neither did working in the library. I hadn't been at school for a long while, not since my postgraduate literature degree. Nor had I expected to go back. Yet my new life—from studying magic to learning my way around the odd dimensions of the library itself—was so much of an improvement on my old life as a bookshop assistant for a boss who cared little for my value as an employee that I couldn't imagine ever returning to that world.

"That'd be good practise for your practical potion-making exam," said Estelle. "I can do it instead, though, if you'd rather take tonight off."

"If you like." I smiled at her. "I still have to practise for next week's familiar exam, so I'm not taking the evening off. That won't involve writing anything, though."

"I'm surrounded by boring overachievers," Sylvester bemoaned.

"Then why not hang out with Cass instead?" I enquired.

Cass rarely came downstairs to help with running the library voluntarily. More often than not, she was to be found behind the door of the Magical Creatures Division up on the third floor, where she smuggled vulnerable and often dangerous magical creatures into the library to look after. Since Cass much preferred animals to people, that worked out in all our favours.

My phone buzzed with a message from my boyfriend, Xavier. *How'd it go?*

Good. My reply probably wouldn't get through for a while thanks to the library's habit of scrambling phone signals, but if past experience was anything to go by, the Grim Reaper's apprentice would already be on his way to the library.

"Xavier?" Estelle guessed, eyeing my phone. "You two should go out tonight. The weather's nice, for a wonder."

"I'll see whether he's free." The notion of taking the night off was certainly appealing, despite the looming prospect of another exam next week that I hadn't done enough preparation for yet. I'd impulsively put myself in for the Grade Three magical exams early so I could take them at the same time as the academy students and had consequently had to cram several years' worth of knowledge into only a couple of months. The fact that the other students taking those exams were younger than nine had not made it any less gruelling, especially as I was also working full-time at the library. As for Xavier's own schedule, Reapers never really got to take days off.

"He'll be free unless someone bites it," Sylvester supplied.

"I'm aware of that, Sylvester, but there's no reason his boss can't handle it instead."

Not that the Grim Reaper would agree. He might have taken a step back from interfering in
our relationship, for a wonder, but that didn't mean he was *happy* about Xavier and me spending time together. The Grim Reaper seemed to be avoiding me altogether these days, though that might have been less due to my relationship with his apprentice and more because I'd recently discovered that he might have met my dad before I'd ever known the magical world existed.

My late father's secrets hadn't come to light until the journal he'd kept throughout my childhood had drawn the attention of a group of vampires known as the Founders and my secret family had come to my rescue. Now the vamps in question were safely ensconced behind bars, I was making steady progress reading through my dad's journal entries, and it had become abundantly clear that while my dad had exiled himself from the magical world to marry my mother, he'd kept the habit of wading into magical intrigue. He might have given up his wand, but his unending fascination for old books had remained intact, and that passion had landed him in the crosshairs of the Founders. Vampires traded in knowledge, and learning the extent of my dad's history with them would have to wait until after my exams were done.

A knock came from the library's front door, which I opened to reveal Xavier standing on the other side. When one heard the words 'Grim Reaper's apprentice,' a devastatingly handsome guy with blond hair and aquamarine eyes was not the image that came to mind, but Xavier wasn't typical of the average Reaper in any way. He was thoughtful, kind, sensitive, caring… and all mine.

I greeted him with a hug and kiss, which prompted a

gagging noise in the background from Sylvester. Ignoring the owl, I said, "It's great to see you."

"Want to head outside?" Xavier asked with a glance at Sylvester. "I bet you need fresh air after being in a stuffy exam room all day."

"I like the sound of that." Considering how rarely the sun showed its face here in Ivory Beach, I needed to soak up all the rays of sunshine I could before it hid itself behind the clouds again. "Typical that the weather is like this when everyone's trapped indoors studying. I'm guessing the Grim Reaper isn't a fan?"

"He's drawn all the curtains in the house."

I grinned at the mental image of the Grim Reaper hiding from the sunshine in a darkened room. "So, business as usual, then."

Xavier and I walked hand in hand across the town square and down a narrow road past the clock tower to reach the seafront. When I'd moved to Ivory Beach last winter, I hadn't exactly arrived at the best time of year for enjoying the beach. Even with the sun's rays caressing the streets, a cool breeze blew off the coast, but a number of bobbing heads were visible in the ocean. Academy students blowing off steam between exams, I guessed. When you lived on the coast in England, you took what you could get—and Ivory Beach was visually appealing even when overcast.

A wide, sandy beach spread as far as the eye could see, with a short pier extending out into the glittering ocean beyond. Xavier and I found a bench to sit on and watch the waves while we caught up on the last few days since we'd seen one another, which did not involve much on my part except studying.

"You don't actually want me to describe the entire exam, do you?" I asked him. "Because that's pretty much been my entire week."

"Still more interesting than mine," he said. "Not that I'm *technically* supposed to confide the details of my Reaper training, but it's just plain boring, to be honest."

"Or a downer," I added. "There's a reason Reapers don't typically entertain at children's birthday parties."

He grinned. "You aren't wrong. Personally, I'd rather hear about your exams than the misery of the recently dead."

That was fair enough. Xavier's main job was to collect the souls of the departed and help them to the next world. I wouldn't call that *boring*, but the magical world had different standards, and a lot of it was still novel to me.

When the weather started to cool down, we retreated to the walkway that ran along the seafront and walked towards the pier to admire the view of the ocean. As I took my first step onto the wooden planks, I glanced down and spotted several oddly shaped gouges in the wooden surface. They formed the outline of what appeared to be two large claws or footprints as if some massive beast had gripped the edge of the pier with all its strength.

"What's that?" I indicated the markings. "Those are far too big to belong to a seagull."

"I haven't a clue," said Xavier. "They definitely don't belong to a mermaid either."

"A werewolf?" I suggested. Did werewolves enjoy swimming? Vampires most certainly didn't. As for the alternatives... Cass was the expert on magical monsters, not me, and I dreaded to think of any of her favourite beasties making their home in the water this close to the beach.

Xavier took a step back. "Maybe we should warn the people who are swimming if they haven't seen."

Good point. The handful of students in the water didn't seem to have noticed the claw marks, but it was better to forewarn them in case whatever the marks belonged to turned out to be something they needed to worry about.

I followed Xavier away from the pier, my gaze briefly lingering on the police station. Would Edwin appreciate us pestering him over a couple of claw marks that might not belong to anything dangerous? I didn't know, but if I were in the water, I'd definitely want to be warned.

Xavier approached the beach. "I can walk into the water myself and tell them, no problem."

As a Reaper, he could even fully immerse himself in the water without needing to breathe, but it never failed to alarm me when I saw him do things that would kill a regular person. Luckily, the students spotted us waving before he entered the water, and a blond girl wearing a polka dot bikini came wading out of the sea onto the beach.

"What is it?" She picked up a towel from the sand and wrapped it around herself. "Ah—you're the Reaper?"

"That's me," said Xavier. "I wondered whether you'd noticed those claw marks over on the pier. We wanted to warn you in case there's something in the water."

She spun towards the pier, dropping her towel. "Whoa. Thanks for warning me. I'll tell the others."

After she hurried away to find her friends, Xavier and I watched until they began to return to shore. Once everyone was safely on the sand, we returned to the walkway.

"I guess nobody else noticed," I remarked to Xavier. "Otherwise, they'd have told the police."

"I think we should do that ourselves," he replied. "When it gets dark, they won't be able to see if there's anything dangerous in the water."

"Yeah, you're right."

It wasn't going to make us very popular with the locals if we got the beach shut down, but having the police back us up ought to stop the complaints if we turned out to be right. On impulse, I darted back to the pier and snapped a picture of the claw marks using my phone so I'd have proof to take to Edwin.

That done, Xavier and I entered the small brick building that housed the local police station and found Edwin talking to one of the large trolls who worked as his assistants. The elf policeman's face took on a familiar long-suffering expression as if he knew we'd come bringing bad news.

"Aurora." He turned towards us. "And the Reaper. Am I right in thinking you've come to report a dead body?"

"It's nothing that serious… I don't think," I added hastily. "We found these weird claw marks on the pier. Whatever they belong to, it's pretty big, and might be dangerous."

"Claw marks?" he echoed. "From what?"

"That's what I'd like to know." I pulled out my phone and showed him. "I don't recognise them, but if they belong to something that might attack people in the water, then people need to be warned."

He squinted at the image. "Is that kelpie back again?"

"Kelpies don't have claws. They have hooves." My cousin Cass had successfully tamed the kelpie in question, though he'd caused a fair bit of chaos a few months ago when he'd escaped his cage and gone rampaging around the library. I knew for a fact that she still paid him the occasional visit, but those gouge-like claw marks weren't the kelpie's.

Edwin glanced up from the phone. "I'll send someone to check it out."

"Thanks, Edwin."

Once we'd left the police station, I turned to Xavier. "Want to head to the Black Dog and grab dinner? I'm supposed to study for my next exam tonight, but I have time to get something to eat first."

"Sure," he said. "Which exam is that again?"

"Familiar training." I led the way to the cosy seafront pub that had become our favourite place to spend our evenings. "I haven't even started proper revision yet."

"Ah," said Xavier, entering the pub behind me. "How's Jet taking it?"

"He seems happy enough, but I'm not sure he actually knows what an exam *is*." My crow familiar, Jet, had been at my side since my arrival in the magical world. A few months ago, I'd tried to put a spell on him to enable easier communication and accidentally given him the ability to talk, which might have given us an advantage in our exam if he hadn't been as excitable as a hyperactive squirrel and prone to getting distracted.

"I'm sure he'll figure it out," Xavier said. "He's good at obeying you when he remembers to listen."

"I only have a week to prepare, so I hope he gets the hang of it fast." I picked out a seat at our usual table in the corner, where Xavier drew less attention than he did elsewhere. The Reaper's apprentice might have been undeniably gorgeous, but he was also unavailable by the very definition of his job, and for that reason, we attracted a lot of stares when we went out together.

"Is this your last exam?" he asked.

"Yeah, and I didn't have many options, short of learning to fly on a broom in the space of a week. Or asking Sylvester to help, which might be worse."

His brows rose. "Would Sylvester help you, do you think? If you bribed him, I mean."

"I guess he did help my cousins back when it was their turn." Granted, they'd been kids, and I was pretty sure he hadn't been capable of talking at the time either. That didn't mean I was desperate enough to beg the owl to help me with my exams. He'd laugh in my face and then give me bogus advice for maximum amusement.

Riding a broomstick was one of the few parts of the magical world that didn't appeal to me. I much preferred casting spells with my feet on the ground, but using a wand was just one part of my magical education, and I needed to master a range of skills to prove myself capable as a witch. That included training my familiar. While convincing Jet to keep calm for the duration of an exam seemed a tall order, it couldn't be worse than asking for Sylvester's help, right?

2

After our date, Xavier dropped me off outside the library, where I kissed him goodbye, regretting having to part ways so early. On our walk home, we'd seen a couple of Edwin's trolls heading out for the pier, but they didn't seem to have put up any signs warning people to stay out of the water. Maybe they were still checking the situation out.

Pushing open the front door, I walked into the library's downstairs floor, set up for the evening with floating lanterns casting an ambient light over the wooden shelves and the tiered balconies overlooking the ground floor. The front desk was closed for the day, but a familiar pair of owl eyes blinked at me from the shadows.

"Where is that boyfriend of yours?"

"He went home. Have you seen Jet?"

"The crow is probably chattering away to your Aunt Candace. Or perhaps he's got himself lost in the Dimensional Studies corridor."

"You wouldn't have anything to do with that, would you?"

The owl gasped. "I cannot believe you would suggest such a thing."

"You've done it before, remember?"

"That crow is not a responsible familiar," said Sylvester. "If he doesn't show up for your exam, I would be glad to take his place... for the right payment."

"Yeah, right." I dreaded to think what trying to do obedience exercises with Sylvester would look like. I'd almost sooner go swimming with whatever monster was lurking around the pier. "That won't be necessary. Jet and I have got this."

As if conjured up by the mere thought of monsters in the water, Cass stepped out from behind a nearby bookcase and addressed the owl. "You only behaved during *my* exam because my mother threatened to lock you up in the Magical Artefacts Division if you didn't. I remember."

"I'm surprised he agreed at all," I remarked. "I thought maybe you volunteered one of your magical creatures instead."

"I tried. My mother wouldn't let me."

Sylvester cackled. "Oh yes. You brought that boggart in, didn't you?"

Cass scowled. "He was well-trained. I still don't get what the problem was."

She'd tried to take her exam with a boggart? I could imagine how the examiners had reacted given that boggarts tended to creep most people out.

"I suppose at least it wasn't a manticore," I said. "Or a kelpie. Let me guess, you hadn't found one yet."

Cass shrugged. "There's a limit to what you can learn in a classroom anyway. Books can't teach you everything."

"Speaking as someone who lives in the biggest magical library in the region." I didn't know whether any others existed since the library was a unique creation of my late grandmother, a product of a manifestation curse that had transformed an ordinary family library into the maze of wonders that we currently inhabited.

"There's more than books in here," Cass said to me. "You ought to know that by now."

"Yes, I'm aware." The library's secrets filled countless rooms, from collections of old artefacts to the vampire who lay sleeping in the basement and had been there for years. He wasn't even the library's sole vampire inhabitant, though my best friend, Laney, was considerably more active.

Cass headed for the corridor leading to our family's living quarters. "I don't know where your familiar is, but I'm guessing Aunt Candace has him passing on gossip for her to use in her latest book."

That figured. "Before you go, I have a question."

Cass halted. "What?"

Pulling out my phone, I showed her the picture of the claw marks I'd found on the pier. "Ever seen those before?"

"Is that our pier?" She studied the image with her eyes narrowed. "You took that today?"

"Yes, but Xavier and I didn't know what the marks belonged to. I thought you might since magical beasts are kind of your area of expertise."

She grunted. "I'd have to see them up close to make a comparison."

"Hang on a second." I put my phone away when she turned towards the door. "You're not going out there right now, are you?"

"Why shouldn't I?"

I shrugged. "It's getting dark, and it's also clear that whatever those claws belong to pulled itself *out* of the water. You don't want to run into it, do you?"

"Absolutely."

"Cass."

A faint rustling noise sounded, and another voice spoke. "What claws?"

Both Cass and I watched as Laney glided out of the corridor to the family's living quarters with the silent grace of a vampire. She'd had an even steeper learning curve in the magical world than me, but she'd coped surprisingly well, and her transformation had also gone a long way towards soothing my initial fear of vampires.

She flashed me a fanged smile. "Hey, Rory. Enjoy your date?"

"Sure." I watched Cass out of the corner of my eye, seeing her mouth twist into a scowl.

Laney pretended to ignore the brewing hostility, though her mind-reading talent meant nobody's intentions were hidden from her. "Go on, tell me about your mysterious clawed creature. Give me all the details."

"There are no details except that it has claws." I pulled out my phone and showed her the photo. "Xavier and I found those claw-marks on the pier earlier. I think the police have already been for a look, but even Cass doesn't know what they belong to."

"I can think of a dozen possible things it *could* be," Cass retaliated. "I need to see it for myself, though."

"You want to risk getting eaten?" Laney shrugged. "Up to you, then."

"Most magical creatures are less dangerous than the average vampire." Cass looked her up and down. "I imagine blood-suckers see anything that feeds on people as a rival predator."

Laney's casual air vanished. "What did you just call me?"

"Hey!" I stepped between them, ignoring Sylvester's eager expression in the background. "Stop it. What's wrong with you two?"

While Cass and I had initially been opposed to one another and we'd never be close friends, her reaction to Laney was on another level. They were constantly bickering for reasons I couldn't figure out, considering I had far more reason to be wary around someone who took lessons from Evangeline, the leader of the town's vampires and one of the people I trusted the least in the entire magical world so far.

"There's nothing wrong with me," Cass said through gritted teeth. "The problem is with *her*."

"You baited her, Cass," I pointed out, but she was no longer paying any attention to me. Turning her back on the door, she marched into the corridor to the living quarters and stomped upstairs. A flutter of wings from the shelves told me that Sylvester had taken off, no doubt disappointed that the fight he'd been hoping to watch hadn't materialised.

Laney watched her leave, her expression unreadable. I turned towards her. "Sorry. I don't know what her problem is."

Laney shrugged, her nonchalant demeanour back. "I unnerve her, I think."

"Are you sure?" Cass didn't like to show her feelings, but it was hard to hide anything from a mind-reading vampire—which was one understandable reason my cousin preferred to stay out of Laney's way. "I guess you're the mind reader, so you'd know."

"I try not to make a habit of dipping into her thoughts —same as all of you," she said. "I'm still learning control, but I think she's paranoid that I'll root out her deepest secrets. As if I care *that* much. I can tell what she thinks of me just by looking at her face, besides."

"Yeah, she's not exactly subtle with her hostility." I trusted Laney, despite it all, but I could understand why Cass didn't. Yet her lack of acceptance of my best friend's presence in the library seemed to go beyond Laney's outsider status, especially as Cass had never had a particular issue with the other vampires.

"I'm used to her by now," she said. "Never thought I'd get used to living in a magical library in a town full of witches and vampires, but there you have it."

"Let's not add 'mystery monsters' to the list if we can avoid it," I added. "Which might well happen if Cass decides to adopt it."

"I can chase it off first."

"I don't think a giant sea monster would much care if you had fangs or not if it wanted to take a bite out of you."

Her pointed teeth became visible when she grinned. "I can run faster than anything except another vampire."

She was probably right on that one. "To be honest, I'd still choose to go up against a mystery monster over Evangeline."

Laney's cavalier attitude to danger was nothing new, but now that she was functionally immortal, her habit of risk-taking had reached new heights. Still, she knew better than to trust the leading vampire, despite being forced to spend her evenings in Evangeline's company, and I tried not to spend too much time worrying about her.

"I'll be fine," Laney said. "Anyway, I'd better go to my lesson. Don't want to keep Her Deadly Elegance waiting."

I snorted at the new nickname. "Please don't let her hear you thinking that."

"Don't worry. I've been learning some new tricks to keep her out of my thoughts."

Before I could ask what those tricks were, she was gone in a blink, through the door and out into the night. Standard for a vampire, but three months ago, she'd been an ordinary human. Having to adjust to being another species altogether was no joke, and I was impressed at how well she'd kept it together. Being able to live with my family in the library had helped, despite Cass's unfriendliness.

The laws of the magical world stated that sharing its secrets with outsiders was forbidden, and I'd taken a major risk when I'd first invited Laney to stay. At the time I hadn't known she'd already been exposed to the magical world, or that she'd landed on Evangeline's radar by taking it upon herself to hunt down several vampires who'd been plotting to kill me. When she'd ended up being bitten by a rogue vamp, Evangeline had offered to give her lessons in exchange for keeping her from facing retaliation from the other vampires—which sounded like a fair deal to anyone unaware of Evangeline's ulterior motives. Namely, her ongoing scheme to find out the contents of my dad's journal, either by reading my mind or reading Laney's. Laney herself was playing a dangerous game by trying to dodge the leading vampire's attempts to wring information from her thoughts, but she had little choice in the matter.

With Jet presumably entertaining himself by chattering to my aunt, I might be better off getting an early night after all, so I could sleep off the stress of the exam and wake up with a clear head. Regardless of my family and friends' decisions, this wasn't the time to get distracted by vampires. Or mystery monsters either.

The next morning, Sylvester woke me up by humming the *Jaws* theme in my ear. I retaliated by swatting at him with my pillow while he retreated in a storm of feathers. I could have sworn I'd locked my door against him, but when the owl wanted to get somewhere, there wasn't much I could do to keep him out. At least Jet respected my privacy. I found my familiar downstairs in the kitchen, talking to Aunt Candace.

"There you are," I said to my familiar. "Want to practise for the exam later when we're done with breakfast?"

"Of course, partner!" he squeaked. "Your aunt is working on a new mystery novel, and now she's heard the news from last night, she wants to put that into the book as well."

"News from last night?" I turned to my aunt. "Is there something I should know?"

"Very intriguing news." Aunt Candace sipped at her

coffee, a knowing glint in her eye. "A group of students claimed to have been chased off by some kind of monster when they were partying on the beach."

"The police didn't put up a sign?" Considering they'd been perfectly aware of the claw marks on the pier, I'd thought they would want to forewarn anyone who wanted to go for a midnight swim. "What kind of monster?"

"Sounds to me like you already know." Aunt Candace put down her coffee mug. "Don't you?"

"No," I replied. "Xavier and I spotted some weird claw marks on the pier yesterday evening, but I don't know what they belonged to."

She huffed. "And you didn't tell me?"

"No, because Cass already tried to run off to check them out, and so did Laney."

Aunt Candace grabbed another piece of toast. "I'm disappointed in you, Rory."

"The police were supposed to put up a sign," I said ineffectually.

She ignored me and left the kitchen at speed, then Cass entered a moment later. "Where's she off to in such a hurry?"

"The pier," I replied. "Our mystery monster scared a few students who were partying on the beach last night so she's off to poke around for a story."

"Really, now." She grabbed a piece of toast of her own. "I'll see whether it left any clearer prints this time."

She left, too, while I looked down at my familiar. "I'm starting to think I'm the only sane one here. Have you seen Estelle or Aunt Adelaide?"

"Estelle said there was a flood up on the first floor," the little crow squeaked. "They're probably dealing with that."

I checked the time. The library wouldn't open for a while and knowing the lengths to which Aunt Candace would go for a good story and Cass's fixation on magical creatures, there was no telling what kind of trouble they might get into if someone didn't check up on them. "Jet, do you want to go to the beach? We can practise some commands on the way."

"Of course, partner!"

I'd expected Cass to get curious enough to have a poke around, but I hadn't counted on the mystery monster making an actual appearance overnight. I wouldn't put it past her to strike up a friendship—or worse, let it come to live in the library. It wouldn't be the first time she'd befriended a dangerous beast, but that didn't mean I needed to leave her to it.

While we walked to the seafront, I practised giving Jet basic instructions to follow, sending him flying in circles or ordering him to collect seashells from the beach. Sometimes he succeeded, and other times he got distracted eavesdropping on people's conversations. It would be different when the two of us were shut in an exam room, but we'd made progress.

Upon reaching the pier, I spied Cass nearby, having removed her cloak and rolled up her trouser legs to wade into the sea.

"What are you doing?" I peered down over the pier's edge to speak to her. "You might have changed into appropriate swimwear first, you know."

"I'm not swimming." She waded out from underneath

the pier, resting a hand on the moss-covered wooden support beam. "What are you doing here?"

"I'd like to know what that creature is too," I answered. "Where are those students who saw it?"

"I don't really care, to be honest," she replied. "I'm more interested in the beast. I think it's a rare aquatic magical mammal."

"Not a werewolf having a nighttime swim, then?"

"Very funny."

"Where'd Aunt Candace go, then?" I didn't see her on the pier, or on the beach either.

"She went to talk to the police."

I groaned. Typical. Backing away from the pier, I approached the police station. Aunt Candace's voice drifted out through the automatic doors, followed by Edwin's exasperated replies, and I sensed his need for my intervention. There'd been an unfortunate incident a few months ago where Aunt Candace had purposefully got herself locked in jail for research purposes and nearly given the poor elf a nervous breakdown.

The automatic doors slid open, and I walked into the police station. "Aunt Candace," I called to her. "I'm pretty sure the police know as much as we do about this mystery monster. Meaning nothing. Come on, let's go back to the library."

"That isn't what I was asking about," she said. "I have some questions for research, you know. It's very important that I know the exact procedure for hunting down and trapping a magical beast to include in my next book."

"The procedure is to ask an expert, not me," Edwin told her. "I'd suggest asking at the local familiar shop."

"Maybe I will." Aunt Candace gave me a wounded

look. "Honestly, Rory, nobody here has any sense of curiosity."

"Cass does, and she's currently wading in the water," I replied. "Edwin, did the students come here to report the attack?"

"Not you too," Edwin said. "I don't have time to answer all your questions."

Aunt Candace began to argue, but I snagged her arm, reluctant to see her get us both into hot water with the police. "If you really want to know that badly, you can always interview the students yourself. I imagine it'd be a novelty for them after spending weeks revising for exams."

She sighed. "I *suppose*, then."

To my intense relief, she came with me without arguing. I cast a glance around the pier for Cass and spied her walking away from the pier. What appeared to be a pile of raw meat lay in the spot where she'd been standing, next to the wooden beam.

I halted in front of her and gestured at the pier. "Did you put that there?"

Cass folded her arms across her chest. "If I said yes, would it get rid of you faster?"

"Were you leaving out bait for the monster?" I didn't really need to ask. "Cass, you can't intentionally attract a possibly lethal and dangerous monster to the beach. It might attack someone."

She shrugged. "It didn't harm anyone last time. Besides, if I feed it, it's less likely to go after the next person who comes here."

"How can you possibly know that?" I glanced over my shoulder at the police station. "Be sensible, Cass. It's not just your own safety at risk."

"There's no law against feeding the birds, is there?"

"Cass." I knew better than to try to change her mind, though. "If you get arrested or eaten, then it's your funeral."

Regardless of what Cass did, the mystery monster was already here, and if past experience was anything to go by, the trouble would inevitably end up back at the library sooner or later. It always did.

3

I lost track of Aunt Candace somewhere on the way back to the library, but I assumed she'd gone to hound Alice at the familiar shop about the process for capturing a deadly beast. I left her to it since I didn't have time to supervise her *and* Cass while they ran around hoping to catch a glimpse of this mystery monster.

Instead, my priority needed to be preparing for my familiar exam. Jet needed the practise more than I did because he couldn't seem to keep himself from excitedly chattering to me about any topic that came to mind.

"You have to be on your best behaviour during the exam," I told him as we walked across the lower floor of the library. "No talking unless it has to do with the subject of the exam. It's not very fun, but it's necessary. Think you can do that?"

"Yes, partner!"

I hoped he'd be able to keep it together. Aunt Adelaide wouldn't be allowed to assess me, so Jet and I would have to impress someone I'd never met before, and who wouldn't find his chattering endearing.

I found an empty classroom to practise in and got out the textbook for the exam. Jet flew in excited circles around the ceiling while I set up the room to mimic the layout of our exam, with various items lying around for him to collect at my command. Most of the tasks would be simple obedience exercises, but my instructions had a tendency to fly in one ear and out the other, and Jet's focus only worsened with time. We'd managed an hour of practise before Sylvester decided to interrupt by rattling the doorknob. "The students are throwing a party!"

"Can't you stop them?" I called back.

"They're very loud!" he shouted. "I can't make myself heard."

I had my doubts given the talents Sylvester had at his disposal, but he was even less susceptible to instructions than Jet was. "Fine, I'll be out in a minute."

I called down my familiar, who perched on the desk in front of me.

"Jet, stay there," I told him. "If you're in the same position when I get back, I'll give you a treat. Think you can do that?"

"Yes, partner!"

The instant I'd left the classroom's soundproofed walls behind, the booming sound of a speaker reached my ears from where someone had set it up near the study tables at the back of the library. Raising my wand, I levitated the speaker into the air and caught it in one hand. A chorus of disappointed cries arose from among the students when I switched off the music.

"No partying in the library," I told them. "I shouldn't have to say that, should I?"

"It was only a bit of music," grumbled a teenage girl who was dressed more like she was on her way to a party than a studying session. "Give that back."

I held up the speaker. "I'm confiscating this for as long as you stay here in the library. If you want it back, you'll have to leave."

"Fine." She sauntered over to me. "We'll leave."

Snatching the speaker from my hand, she tottered away on her heeled shoes. Her friends followed, muttering about boring people ruining the fun. I ignored their complaints, which were nothing new. I'd spent my own teenage years studying for my exams rather than going out clubbing. As an undergraduate, Laney had convinced me to go clubbing with her a couple of times, but she hadn't minded that I'd preferred a quiet evening in with a book to a sweaty, noisy room where everyone was drunk and nobody could hear each other speak.

Once the students had left, I attempted to return to the classroom where I'd left Jet, only to find that Spark the pixie had got into the room and was chasing my familiar around in circles.

Getting the message, I gave up on familiar training for the time being and went to help Estelle at the front desk instead. Cass was nowhere to be seen, and when I asked Estelle, she said she hadn't seen her come back from the beach. That wasn't typical of her given her liking for locking herself up away from human contact most of the time. Same with Aunt Candace, come to that.

"Where's Aunt Adelaide?" I asked next.

"Still dealing with that flood upstairs," Estelle replied. "It was caused by a leaking water pipe, apparently."

I arched a brow. "Are you sure? That seems a bit mundane for the library. Unless that mystery monster is trying to swim through the plumbing."

Estelle shuddered. "Rory, you're as bad as Aunt Candace."

"She actually did write that in a book, you know."

"Of course she did." Estelle shook her head. "She doesn't need to bombard the police with questions to get book ideas."

"I hope she's given up on that by now."

Belatedly, it occurred to me that some of the students here might have been at the beach yesterday or witnessed the "mystery monster" attack the previous night. I ought to have seized my chance to ask when I'd confiscated their music.

"Me too," said Estelle. "Weren't you and Jet practising for your exam?"

"Until Sylvester interrupted and Spark started chasing Jet around."

"So, that's where he went," she said. "I can fetch him."

"Nah, I'll do it," I said. "I wanted to have a word with the students anyway."

"Don't tell me you're taking a leaf out of Aunt Candace's book and asking about that monster."

"I'm not going to try to befriend or interview it, don't worry. I just want to know what it is so I can be mentally prepared."

"Fair enough," she said. "Sure, go ahead."

Wishing I'd thought of the idea sooner, I headed for the students' corner of the library again and approached a table of quiet, studious-looking pupils dressed in uniforms.

"Sorry to bother you," I said to them. "I wondered whether any of you heard about the incident at the beach last night?"

A girl wearing glasses decorated with tiny pixies briefly looked up. "Who didn't?"

"Was anyone here involved?" I asked her.

"Sure," she answered. "You know those people who you just threw out for playing music?"

Oh no. "Seriously? All of them were there?"

"Some of them." She shrugged. "I bet they were making it up. They were drunk anyway."

"I saw the claw marks on the pier yesterday myself."

"You did?" A guy with an unfortunate amount of acne on his forehead looked at me with an expression of interest.

"Doesn't mean that's what *they* saw," the girl with pixie glasses insisted. "That Marla Hutchins makes up stories all the time."

"All right. I just wondered what the general opinion is." Since the actual witnesses weren't around, I wasn't likely to learn anything new from anyone here. "Thanks for talking to me."

"We're glad you confiscated that speaker," the girl added. "And kicked them out. Now we can actually study."

"No problem." At least someone was grateful to me for maintaining the peace. Really, it wasn't like the students didn't already have enough places to throw parties and otherwise get distracted. Like the beach, for instance.

After I fetched Spark the pixie, I joined Estelle at the front desk and waited for Aunt Candace and Cass to return with news. Aunt Candace came into the library first, grumbled something about rude students, and then walked away without answering any of our questions.

Cass, however, took much longer to come back. It wasn't until we were closing the library for the night that my cousin entered the lobby. She must have used a drying spell on her clothes since she'd been dripping wet the last time I'd seen her.

"Hey," I said when she came marching past the desk. "Any signs of the mystery monster?"

"Not yet. I'm going out tonight, though, so maybe it'll come out after dark."

"No, you aren't," Aunt Adelaide said from the balcony. "You're going to help me deal with this flood."

Cass tutted. "Ask Rory instead."

"Rory has an exam to study for."

I did—which meant no date with Xavier tonight, unfortunately. With only a few days until my exam, I needed the extra time to practise with Jet, preferably without any interruptions this time around. Including from mystery monsters.

The following day, I woke to what sounded like a landslide. I emerged from my room as Aunt Candace came sailing downstairs in her dressing gown as if she'd won the lottery.

"What's going on?" I called to her.

"What makes you think something is going on?" she shouted up from below.

I clattered downstairs to join her in the living room.

"The fact that you're voluntarily up this early, for one thing."

"I smelled a story," she announced. "It woke me up."

"Are you sure it isn't the stack of plates you've had in your room for the past week?" Aunt Adelaide poked her head around the corner. "I told you to bring them into the kitchen."

"Hilarious." Aunt Candace gave us both a withering look. "There's mischief afoot, and I intend to find its source."

She swept off into the main part of the library without another word, and I swivelled to face Aunt Adelaide. "How did she even hear about this 'story'?"

The answer came flying downstairs in a storm of black feathers. Jet, it seemed, had been awake in the early hours of the morning hunting down gossip. No wonder he couldn't focus on our practise sessions. He flew straight past me in pursuit of Aunt Candace, who'd left through the library's front door.

"Should I go with her?" I asked uncertainly.

"Oh, go ahead," said Aunt Adelaide. "We might as well be prepared for whatever madness she brings back to the library next."

She wasn't wrong. At least Cass didn't seem to be downstairs, but if the news turned out to be related to our mystery monster, she wouldn't be far behind.

I went upstairs to properly dress before leaving the library myself. There was no point in trying to chase Aunt Candace down while she was running at full speed, and unlike her, I had zero desire to go to the beach in my pyjamas or dressing gown. Instead, I dressed in jeans and a T-shirt and grabbed the black cloak embossed with our family's coat of arms, which depicted an owl sitting atop two crossed pens. Shrugging on my cloak, I picked up my bag and then headed back downstairs.

When I opened the front door, the sea breeze brought the sound of a commotion from the seafront. I hurried across the square and found a crowd of at least twenty or thirty people gathered around the pier, where Edwin's troll guards were attempting to keep order.

It was easy to see what had drawn their attention. A sizeable chunk appeared to be missing from the pier's end as if something had either bitten or chewed through the wood. My aunt stood talking to one of the troll guards while Edwin hid behind another. I didn't blame him in the slightest given my aunt's dishevelled state and wild eyes. Not to mention the notebook floating at her side. The rest of the crowd were equally keen to get a look, but their path to the pier remained blocked by a wall of trolls. Edwin's giant guards, being too heavy to stand on the pier without causing even more damage to the wooden planks, formed a barrier that even my aunt couldn't surpass. The other onlookers gave up a few at a time, and I stayed near the back until the crowd had dispersed enough for me to have a proper look at the pier.

The creature had apparently used its teeth or claws to tear the end of the pier clean off, leaving splintered pieces of wood littering the water. I wouldn't like to meet whatever was responsible for causing that level of destruction, but when I peered over the edge, I noted that the bait Cass had left underneath the pier was no longer there. That didn't mean the monster had devoured it, though, but had Cass been responsible for it coming back after all?

As the crowd thinned out, none other than Cass

herself approached from the side street. Unlike our aunt, she had at least put clothes on first, with her hair tied back and her most sternly antisocial expression plastered on.

"Hey," I said to her. "You didn't come out again last night, did you?"

"No. If I had, I'd have seen this." She indicated the splintered remains of the pier's end.

"Or you'd have got yourself eaten. You can't run as fast as a vampire, remember?"

"The creature wouldn't eat me. I left it some bait, remember?"

"You did *what?*" A snooty-looking blond guy in a pressed suit marched over to us, looking Cass up and down. "Did you say *you* left the bait that drew this dangerous monster to the beach?"

"Who might you be?" Cass gave him an equally disdainful look right back. "The police?"

"Actually, yes. I'm here from Wildwood Heath, and—"

"He's on holiday," interrupted a blond woman with a red squirrel familiar sitting on her shoulder. She looked similar enough to the man for me to guess they were related. "Ignore him."

"She was confessing to a crime," the man said, his face flushing a little. "It's illegal to leave bait for dangerous magical creatures."

"She did what?" asked a passing wizard, eyeing Cass. "I saw you in the water. Making friends with monsters, were you?"

Oh boy. It looked like I hadn't been the only one to notice Cass's shenanigans the previous day. Her eyes narrowed. "Who might you be?"

"A concerned local," the wizard retaliated. "I ought to report you to the police, you know. If you hadn't left out the bait, the creature that wrecked the pier wouldn't have come back."

"Not necessarily true," the blond woman interjected. "Word of advice? Move along before she hexes you."

"Stay out of this," Cass spat at her.

"That was friendly," said the blond woman. "I was standing up for you. You're welcome. C'mon, Ramsey."

The blond man—Ramsey—scowled at the woman, who could only be his sister. "We might be on holiday, but the laws still apply."

"Exactly!" said the "concerned local," who should really have been more concerned about Cass's furious expression than the monster. "You're lucky nobody died."

"Want to volunteer as bait next time?" Cass asked.

"Cass." I grabbed her arm before she seized her wand. "Stop it. Look, the police are watching."

One of Edwin's troll guards had turned in our direction, his knuckles cracking. Seeming to notice him for the first time, Ramsey and his sister stopped in their tracks. The local wizard, meanwhile, glowered at both of us before striding off.

Cass rolled her eyes. "Some people are all bark and no bite."

"Not your mystery monster, though." I dropped my voice. "Did you figure out what it is?"

"You know as much as I do." She scowled. "The cheek of it. I didn't leave bait out so it could come and scare off some students who were stupid enough to throw a party down there on the beach. I put the bait in the sea, besides."

"Was it in the water when it scared them, though? Or did it climb out?"

A flicker of movement at my feet drew my gaze to the pier, where the red squirrel who'd been with the blond woman had slipped past the troll guards. Sniffing at the wooden beams, the squirrel appeared to examine the damage the mystery monster had left behind before returning to where the blond woman waited. As I watched, the squirrel scampered up to her shoulder and leaned close to her ear. Her lips moved, though I didn't hear any words. Were they talking to one another?

"Rory," the nearest troll guard rumbled. "Your cousin has gone. Can you stay away from the pier?"

I spun around. In my brief moment of distraction, Cass had slipped away. Typical.

"Sorry," I said to the troll. "I'll go back to the library."

I hoped Cass had done the same, but Aunt Candace certainly hadn't. I glimpsed her talking to another troll guard as I walked back towards the town square.

When I entered the library, Aunt Adelaide was at the front desk preparing to open for the day. "Where's Candace?"

"Pestering the police in her dressing gown, assuming she's not in a cell."

"Of course she is," said Aunt Adelaide. "Not Edwin, I hope?"

"Nah, she's talking to his troll guards," I replied. "Should I have stopped her?"

"Nobody can stop my sister when she's on a mission," she said. "What's the latest on this mystery creature, then?"

"It chewed off the end of the pier. Or clawed at it. Not sure which."

She winced. "Nobody was hurt, were they?"

"No, but Cass has managed to make a few enemies who overheard her talking about leaving bait out for the creature yesterday."

Aunt Adelaide groaned. "She didn't, did she?"

"Unfortunately, yes."

"I'll have a word with her," she said. "Not that that usually does any good. I thought she might have plans to befriend the creature, but I didn't expect anything like this."

"Neither did I," I admitted. "You'd think someone would be able to identify what it is. There's nothing the library doesn't know, right?"

"Oh, I've no doubt the library knows. It's just a question of whether you're patient enough to find the answers. Or to ask the right question."

If I had to guess, that was a reference to the Book of Questions, otherwise known as the Forbidden Room and the source of Sylvester's knowledge. I could certainly drop in there and ask what the mystery beast was, but whether Sylvester answered was up to him, and we hadn't exactly been getting along particularly well that week. The trick of the Forbidden Room was that each member of my family was permitted to ask one question per day, and if it wasn't phrased in precisely the right way, Sylvester might wriggle out of answering.

Cass had never used the Forbidden Room herself as far as I could tell, but when it came to animals of the magical variety, learning through practical experience was more her style than consulting a book. I didn't think she'd intentionally put others' lives at risk, but Cass's sense of responsibility was outweighed by her insistence on befriending any magical creature that crossed her path. Perhaps even ones that chewed up the pier and chased off the locals.

"Mum!" Estelle called from upstairs. "The corridor has flooded. I think the leak is back."

"Not this again." Aunt Adelaide tutted. "Can you watch the desk, Rory?"

"Sure." I called Jet down to join me, figuring I might as well get in some practise for our upcoming exam while I worked at the desk, though part of me wondered whether I should send him to the beach to keep an eye on my aunt instead. I didn't envy whoever ended up escorting Aunt Candace away from the scene, but those siblings who'd come here on holiday struck me as equally worthy of watching. The woman with the squirrel familiar, certainly. It wasn't every day that I ran into someone who appeared to communicate directly with her familiar. Maybe she could give me tips. If Cass hadn't put her off coming near our family entirely, that is.

"Looks like it's just you and me for now, partner," I remarked to Jet. "Can you fetch me that pen?"

Jet tossed me a pencil, which I caught with a sigh. "Close enough."

4

The rest of the day proceeded more or less as normal, as far as life in the library went. It took most of the morning for Aunt Adelaide to clean up the flood upstairs, which had allegedly been caused by someone throwing a mouse down the sink. Considering exactly one of the library's inhabitants ate rodents, I'd been inclined to blame a certain owl, not that he'd owned up to anything.

Cass remained locked in her usual room on the third floor while Aunt Candace showed no signs of returning to the library. I pitied anyone who had to deal with her constant questions, but I had no free time to rescue them with the number of students coming in and out of the library with requests to help them prepare for their upcoming exams.

Estelle took over for me at lunchtime when Xavier dropped by to ask whether I wanted to go for a walk, which was more than welcome on another sunny day when I'd spent most of my time indoors. We stopped at

Zee's bakery and bought muffins to eat on the walk to the beach.

"Did you hear the latest on our mystery monster?" I asked him.

"I saw the crowd earlier," Xavier commented. "Were you there?"

"Yeah, Aunt Candace went running out to start questioning the police right away," I said. "She's still there, as far as I know. Cass, though… to be honest, she might have been the one who lured the monster back to the pier in the first place. She left out bait yesterday."

His brows rose. "Cass doesn't know what the creature actually is, though, right?"

"If she does, she hasn't enlightened the rest of us."

We reached the seafront to find that the remainder of the crowd had mostly dispersed, with the end of the pier roped off instead of guarded by trolls. The police must have returned to their offices, but given Aunt Candace's absence, that hadn't deterred her from questioning them.

"Poor Edwin," I said. "Aunt Candace has been here for hours. I think she's still in her dressing gown too."

"She must really think she can get a story out of this." He approached the ropes. "I guess they blocked off the pier so nobody else can get any ideas."

"There's not much of it left," I commented. "Given the state of things, I can't tell whether it was even the same creature that left the first set of claw marks."

"I can have a look"—Xavier stepped forward—"though I'd rather avoid getting into trouble with Edwin."

"He's probably hiding from my aunt."

"True." Xavier strode towards the cordoned off area while I watched from the side. Nearby, the original claw marks were still there. The bait Cass had left was gone, of course, but it could as easily have been eaten by some other animal than the intended target. Like her kelpie friend, for instance.

"What do you think?" I called to Xavier.

He halted near the splintered wood at the pier's end and peered at the wreckage. "Hard to tell. It looks like claws did this, not teeth, but I'm not sure it would be much of a reassurance to anyone standing in the way."

"You aren't wrong." I suppressed a shiver. "There are no footprints—or claw-prints, though."

"There might be some in the water." He left the pier and made for the beach instead, descending the gentle slope from the walkway to the sand.

Watching Xavier wade out to sea without being touched by the waves never ceased to be disconcerting. While he was in no danger of being swept up in the currents, I grimaced when the waves lapped around him as he walked underneath the pier to look around the area where the beast had clawed its way to the surface.

A minute later, he emerged out of the sea without so much as a single droplet of water falling off him. That was Reapers for you.

"Find anything?" I asked.

"No." He came to a halt in front of me. "Any prints would have been washed away, I guess."

"And you're sure it was the same creature as this one?" I indicated the first set of claw marks. "If so, then I wonder why it caused so much more damage the second time around."

"We don't know how mystery monsters' minds work."

"Well, no," I acknowledged. "I'm surprised it's stayed a

mystery for this long without someone guessing what it is."

"The police might have."

"If they aren't too busy answering questions from Aunt Candace." The only people who'd actually *seen* the creature were those students, though. I doubted they'd be willing to talk after I'd kicked them out of the library the previous day, but their classmates didn't seem inclined to take their word for it anyway.

Still, I found it hard to believe a monster had caused this level of damage without any witnesses to speak of.

"Didn't she talk to them yesterday as well?" asked Xavier.

"Yes, until Edwin told her to ask at the familiar shop if she wanted to learn about the process of trapping magical mystery monsters instead."

"That's not a bad call," he said. "The familiar shop owner might have an idea of what the creature is."

"Maybe." Alice was one of the town's experts on magical animals, and unlike Cass, she was friendly and willing to answer questions. "I'll ask her on the way back to the library."

"Good idea. I should get back to my boss."

Xavier and I parted ways outside the familiar shop, and I ducked inside. The small red-brick building sat on the northwest corner of the square and was a cosy riot of animal noises. Birds flew back and forth across the ceiling, cats prowled around, and cawing and barking and squeaking filled the background.

Alice herself sat behind the counter, feeding a large bird a long ear of corn. A snake coiled around her neck amid her curly hair, and she gave me a friendly smile when she spotted me enter the shop. "Hey, Rory."

"Hey, Alice. Have you heard the news?"

"The mystery monster?" she guessed. "You're about the tenth person who's asked me—including your aunt. I haven't had time to check out the pier yet, but I've had a bunch of people ask if one of my familiars got out."

"They think a familiar was responsible. Really?" I looked around the shop at the various creatures, which ranged from birds to cats, but saw nothing remotely big enough to have torn through solid wood. "There's nothing in here that has long enough claws to have caused that kind of damage."

"Exactly," said Alice. "They didn't actually accuse me of anything, but I got a few joking questions about whether I was keeping a manticore in the basement."

"That's more Cass's thing."

"Your cousin." She wore a peculiar look on her face. "Yeah, I can see that."

"I didn't know you'd met." Granted, Cass's fixation on magical creatures meant they were bound to have crossed paths at some point.

"We... we kind of dated for a bit."

"You did?" That was news. Estelle had mentioned Cass's recent ex-boyfriend when we'd first met so I'd assumed she'd exclusively dated guys, though that was more of an assumption on my part. Granted, Cass herself was uncommunicative at the best of times, so it shouldn't be surprising that we'd been living in the same building for more than six months and I'd had zero clue of their history with one another.

Alice shrugged. "Yeah. I'm not really surprised she

didn't mention it. She tends to be pretty cagey with the details of her private life. Keeps them locked up tighter than those manticores of hers."

"Tell me about it," I replied. "She left bait out for the creature at the pier, so a few people are ticked off with her and think she lured it back to the beach herself."

Alice blinked. "She didn't, did she?"

"Yep," I said. "Given the damage the mystery monster caused last night, I think it's safe to say it didn't appreciate the gesture."

"Wow," she said. "Yeah. I suppose if there were no witnesses, we can only guess at why it trashed the pier, but from the description of the damage, the creature was likely provoked or distressed. I don't think Cass leaving food out would have brought that on."

"Nobody has owned up to seeing or hearing anything yet, but you'd think someone would have." Someone ought to have heard the noise, especially people who lived near the seafront or were otherwise within hearing distance. "The other night, some students claimed to have seen the creature, but they were drunk at the time and not exactly reliable as eyewitnesses."

"No, I expect that's why your aunt came to talk to me," Alice said. "I gave her the number of an expert to get her out of my hair."

"An expert on mystery monsters?"

"Someone who knows how to capture runaway magical creatures," she clarified. "Not a local one, but it's not a service we typically have need of."

"And if we did?" I asked. "We'd be able to call them in to capture the creature?"

"They'd need to know what they're actually looking

for in order to be of any help," she said. "But honestly, any regular witch or wizard ought to be more than capable of restraining a magical beast. I'd go looking for it myself if I had someone who could watch the shop for me."

"Not everyone has a knack for dealing with magical animals, though, right?" I asked. "I mean, not everyone even has a familiar."

"No, but some are better with them than others," she said. "I had a family of tourists come in here the other day who seemed to really know their stuff. One of them had a red squirrel."

"Oh, I saw her at the beach," I recalled. "Do you think *they* might know what the creature is?"

"I don't know, but they seemed pretty knowledgeable about magical creatures. They arrived in town a couple of days ago."

Hmm. That might be a line of questioning to pursue. Especially given that the mystery monster had struck around the same time as they'd arrived.

"Speaking of familiars, is there a way for me to convince Jet to be more... attentive?" I asked. "We have our familiar exam soon, and he's trying his best, but he's not the best at following instructions. I wondered if you had some tips."

"Ah, that's not an uncommon issue," she said. "Some familiars just don't adapt well to exam settings. Rewards might work, and praise. Tell you what, I have a free booklet with some tips, and I'll throw in a sample of some treats that bird familiars love."

"Good idea." I took the leaflet from her. "Ah, the free sample isn't necessary. I'll pay."

My lunch hour was almost over, so I left the pet shop

laden with bags of treats for my familiar and made straight for the library. At least I had an idea of how to train Jet, despite my lack of progress on the subject of the mystery monster. A nagging sense that I ought to be able to do more persisted despite my efforts to push the subject out of my mind. After all, the library was the town's main source of information on any magic-related topic… or to be more specific, the Book of Questions was.

When I walked into the library, I found Sylvester sitting on the desk as if he'd anticipated that I wanted to consult the book. When he spotted the bag of treats in my hands, he flapped his wings so vigorously he almost knocked over a stack of returns.

"They're not for you," I told him. "They're for Jet. If there are any left after the exam, you can have them."

He huffed at me, his claws splayed across the record book.

"Sylvester, don't sit on that." I tugged the book out from underneath his claws. "I'm guessing you heard the latest news?"

"Repeatedly," said the owl. "If your aunt and cousin get eaten by a monster, it serves them right for meddling."

"Nobody was meddling except for Cass, and I doubt you want *her* to get eaten by the mystery monster." I gave him a look. "She left bait out for the creature. Not sure why it repaid her by tearing up the pier."

Sylvester made a clucking noise. "This is a simple beast you're referring to, not a highly intelligent being like myself."

I snorted. "Can the Book of Questions tell me what kind of creature it is? Or would you have to see the marks for yourself first?"

His wings spread wide. "Don't speak so loudly. You don't know who might be listening."

"Don't be so dramatic." I rolled my eyes. "Is the creature's identity likely to exist within the room, or do I need more information?"

I guessed the latter, but it would help to have some direction aside from a few claw marks and the testimony of a group of drunken teenagers.

When Sylvester didn't answer, I asked, "Cass doesn't use the Forbidden Room, does she?"

"Ask her, not me. I'm not a mind reader... unlike your friend."

"Laney can't read *your* mind, Sylvester."

"And good riddance." He sniffed. "It's impossible to keep secrets in this place anymore."

"Says the library's major source of information, who refuses to answer my questions."

He made a hooting noise of annoyance. "You wound me."

"That wasn't even an insult, Sylvester. It was the truth."

The owl ignored me and took flight, careful to spread his wings wide to hit me over the head on his way past. At least he left the bag of treats alone, though I'd keep them close at hand until the exam was over.

As for the Book of Questions, that was never the easiest option despite its deceptively simple nature. The Book's knowledge covered the library, not that which lay outside of it. Though now that I'd brought up the subject, I wondered whether Cass had ever consulted the Forbidden Room at all. I assumed she didn't know Sylvester's real identity, though Cass was the only one of us Sylvester remotely got along with. Perhaps for that exact reason. Not even a vampire could read the owl's mind, but they could read *mine*, and I didn't like to think of what the potential consequences might be if Evangeline learned Sylvester's secret. No doubt unpleasant ones.

Wishing that particular thought had never crossed my mind, I put down the treats and checked the booklet Alice had given me to help with training Jet. The book began with a brief guide on what kinds of creatures were suitable as familiars. While most people I knew typically choose a cat or a bird, there were other options, though the book cautioned against trying unusual or exotic magical creatures that had a warning label attached. I couldn't help smiling when I imagined how Cass would react if she read it.

According to the book, conventional familiars were the easiest to tame, especially cats, but most of them responded well to being offered treats in exchange for obeying commands. The illustration of a bright-red squirrel brought to mind that family of tourists and the squirrel who'd seemed to communicate with the blond witch as if they could understand each other's speech. Perhaps she'd used a spell like the one I'd used on Jet to make her squirrel able to talk, though I'd used my Biblio-Witch magic on Jet, and the gift was restricted to our family. Granted, it might not be the only way. I'd have to ask, and her brother had acted so rudely that I doubted *he* was willing to stop and chat, let alone answer questions.

I'd have to get her alone first, and then I'd find out whether she knew anything about the mystery monster.

5

As it turned out, though, I didn't have to hunt down the family of tourists myself.

That afternoon, Aunt Candace finally slunk back into the library, still wearing her dressing gown.

"What on earth have you been doing all day?" I asked her as she walked past the desk. "Not pestering Edwin?"

"How insulting," she said. "I have been asking important questions pertaining to my research, not *pestering* anyone as if I were a curious child."

"Of course not," I said. "You're a grown woman who's been outside in her nightclothes all day, asking the police about monsters, not a child."

"Impertinent." She huffed and walked away, disappearing upstairs.

A moment later, the library's door opened, and the blond woman I'd seen at the beach came in. Her red squirrel darted ahead of her and looked up at the library's tiered layers with beady eyes.

"Hey," the blond witch said to me. "I'm Robin. This is

Tansy, my familiar. Sorry we met under weird circumstances earlier. My brother is kind of a stuck-up annoyance."

The squirrel squeaked a greeting and climbed onto her owner's shoulder with her gaze still fixed on the upper floors. Possibly, she was imagining how fun it would be to climb all over the balconies and shelves.

"Ramsey has the verbal equivalent to his hedgehog familiar's spikes," Robin added. "Don't take it personally."

"He has a hedgehog familiar?"

"Named Prickles. I know." She gave the library a once-over. "I like this place. Tansy does too. She said it smells nice."

"That's probably the familiar treats. I was training my crow." I indicated Jet, who was currently snoozing in a ray of sunshine near the window. "Anyway, is there anything I can help you with?"

"I'm looking for information on magic wands… that sort of thing."

I blinked. I'd expected a question on magical creatures, not wands, but if Robin and her family were experts in that subject, then maybe it was to be expected that they'd come to the library to learn about something else altogether.

"Sure," I replied. "That will be on the second floor along with most of the volumes on magical artefacts."

Wand-making was a niche and little-known area, perhaps because there were very few wand-makers in the magical world and they guarded their secrets well. Aunt Adelaide had told me that Ivory Beach got their wands from elsewhere because there were no local experts, but the library ought to have the information they were looking for.

I unfurled the long roll of paper listing the contents of the various floors to check I'd remembered the right one and then rolled it up again.

"I'll lead the way," I told Robin. "I need to find someone to watch the desk first."

Aunt Adelaide must have asked Estelle to help with the leaking pipe, and presumably, Spark the pixie had gone with her. I didn't want to wake up Jet, but I knew better than to ask either of the other two human inhabitants to watch the desk. Which left one option.

"Sylvester," I called out. "Sylvester, can you watch the desk?"

I didn't expect a reply after our altercation earlier, but a flutter of wings heralded Sylvester's arrival. The giant tawny owl flew down to the desk, where he studied Robin with interest. "Hello, there."

Robin blinked in evident surprise that he'd spoken to her. "Oh, hi. You're Sylvester?"

"The one and only." The owl puffed out his chest. "You're new in town."

"Just visiting." Robin eyed him, while her familiar peered out from behind her hair, matching her witch's wariness. "I'm Robin, and this is Tansy."

"We need you to watch the desk," I told Sylvester, "while we're looking up information on wands."

"Why would you want to do that?" The owl addressed Robin. "You have so much raw talent inside your fingertips that a wand is as good as a stick to you."

"Erm... thanks?" Robin said. "It's not regular wands we need to learn about, though. More... sceptres."

"Oh, you'll want the Artefacts Division," he said. "Have you got the key, Aurora?"

"The key to what?"

"The door, of course."

Brow furrowing, I consulted the list. "There's no mention of a key here."

"You need one to get through *that* door." He ducked under the desk and tossed a worn key in my direction, which I caught in my hand. "You're welcome."

"Ah—Sylvester, you can't have that." I snatched the bag of treats from his line of sight. "I told you, not until after the exam."

I hastened away from the desk in case he tried to cuff me again, but the owl simply watched Robin and me head into the Research Division and towards the stairs.

"That was weird," I said in a low voice. "Sylvester doesn't usually talk to our visitors."

"He's your familiar?" She sounded sceptical. "You can hear him talk?"

"So can you... oh." *Oh.* "Most people can't. I mean, he doesn't usually talk to them anyway, but my cousin used a spell on him a few years ago so we can understand him. I thought it only applied to our family."

"It probably does." She glanced around. "My family... we have a special gift when it comes to understanding animals. *All* animals, not just familiars."

"That explains why I saw you talking to Tansy at the beach."

Tansy's red tail flicked up and down, and she made a squeaking noise.

"That's true," Robin confirmed. "Though the owl... he's..."

"He's what?" Sylvester asked from behind us, making both of us startle.

Robin recovered first. "I can usually understand animals when they speak without the need for a spell, that's all."

"All animals?"

"Of course." She smiled at Tansy, who made a chittering noise. Presumably, Robin understood her meaning, even if I didn't. "Comes in handy sometimes."

"I bet." I resumed walking towards the stairs that curved around the library's walls and connected each storey to the one above. "I can understand my crow familiar, too, but that's because I used a similar spell on him."

"So you don't have that gift with all animals, then? I figured someone in my family would have told me if you did."

"No, my family's magical gift involves being able to manipulate words. It comes in handy in its own way, especially in here."

"Neat." She followed me up the staircase. "This place seems fun to live in. Doesn't hurt that you're close to the beach. Tansy hasn't been near the sea in years. Neither have I, for that matter."

There was my opening. "Speaking of the sea, I'm guessing you heard the rumours?"

"That mystery monster?" she guessed. "Does that sort of thing happen often?"

"Not to my knowledge," I replied. "I mean, we've had wild animals come out of the sea, but this time nobody can identify what it is."

"Huh," she said. "Yeah, it struck me as unusual, but I'm not local, so I wasn't sure."

"Would your... ability work on it? The mystery monster, I mean?"

"Sure, if it's an animal."

I frowned. "You mean it might not be?"

My remarks about aquatic shifters came floating back into my mind, but we reached the second floor before she could reply. Robin and Tansy admired the rows of towering shelves while I consulted the list to find the right room. I hadn't been this clueless for a while, thanks to my growing experience in navigating the more commonly used areas of the library, and magical artefacts weren't a subject I typically needed to look up. I'd inherited my dad's old wand and was glad to have it, but I knew more about my Biblio-Witch magic than the mechanics of wands.

"This way." I led Robin through the maze of shelves to a heavily padlocked door. The padlocks were large, silver in colour, and solidly heavy. What were they trying to keep contained? Given the nature of the library, it might be the books themselves or something else entirely. The only way to know for sure was to open the door.

"Is there a particular title that catches your interest?" I pointed out the list of books that was helpfully affixed to the wall next to the door. "Because given the size of those padlocks, we might want to get in and out of that room as fast as possible."

Robin eyed the door. "You don't know what's in there?"

"I only moved here a few months ago," I explained. "Nobody has asked me about wands yet, so this is new territory for me. It can't be as bad as some of the things

I've found in the Vampires or Magical Creatures Sections, but you never really know."

She tilted her head in interest. "I'm surprised this place is legal, to be honest, but I guess it's hard to regulate somewhere that's family-owned. Your family is the leading coven in town, right?"

"We're not exactly a coven. Not by the usual standard." Ivory Beach didn't have any large covens, though the library stood at the centre of town and certainly wasn't the norm either. "If you don't know what book you want, then we can have a look. Just, you might want your wand at the ready."

"Okay." She pulled out her wand, seemingly unfazed, while I used the key to unlock the padlocks on the door.

Robin's lack of fear wasn't necessarily unusual given that she'd evidently grown up in the magical world. Considering her magical gift and the questions she'd asked so far, I guessed she belonged to a particularly influential coven in her own community. Old covens tended to have the strongest magical gifts that lasted through the generations, which was likely why she'd thought my family was a leading coven as well. The truth was, though, I didn't know much of our family history before my grandmother since she'd created the library as it existed today. My ancestors had been librarians, but of the regular sort of library. The type with normal dimensions.

I unlatched the last padlock and pocketed the key. Then I nudged the door inwards and revealed a dark, dusty little room.

"There are only five books in there," Robin observed. "Why go to all that trouble to lock them up?"

I think we're about to find out. Pushing the door open farther, I took a step into the room, one hand on the pocket of my coat containing my Biblio-Witch Inventory.

Tansy scampered ahead of me towards the stack of books in the corner. If I had to guess, she'd volunteered to check for trouble first. Robin followed close behind her and crouched down to examine the books. "Why aren't they shelved?"

Tansy made a squeak of alarm. A grating noise echoed off the walls as the floor began to spin, and the books vanished amid what appeared to be a large cabinet.

"What the—?" Robin broke off, peering at the cabinet. "It has words on it."

I took a step closer. The scrawling writing said, "Don't touch the door or you will be devoured."

"Well... that's instructive." I drew in a breath. "I guess we have to unlock the cabinet without touching it." I pulled out my Biblio-Witch Inventory and tapped the word *unlock*.

The floor spun again, and spikes sprang up out of the walls, extending outwards to face the pair of us. Tansy ran in circles, squeaking in alarm, while the spikes sprang up out of all three walls.

"What is this supposed to be?" Robin asked. "Some kind of medieval torture device?"

"I have no idea, but don't encourage it." I scanned my Biblio-Witch Inventory in the hopes of finding a word that would get rid of the spikes, but none seemed ideal. "If you want to get at the books, I think one of us has to use the right kind of unlocking spell. Otherwise, we get spiked to death."

Robin scrunched her forehead up. "I'm not good at riddles."

"You're good at magic, aren't you?" I pressed. "Sylvester said so, and he doesn't give out praise easily."

"Huh." She raised her wand. "Okay, I'll try a summoning spell to get a book out of the cabinet without touching it."

She flicked her wand. To my alarm, the spikes extended outwards, and Tansy let out an urgent squeak. More spikes had emerged from the floor, forming a jagged path between us and the way out.

"I guess not, then." Robin swore under her breath. "Tansy, what spell might get us past an enchanted cabinet?"

"This is the Artefacts Division." I thought hard. "It's got to be a spell connected to whatever you're looking for."

Her face flushed. "If so, then I didn't bring the right prop with me."

"What do you mean by 'prop'?" I tensed when the spikes jutting from the floor continued to extend upwards like jagged fangs. "I don't think the library is going to let us out until you solve this one."

"I mean the artefact I'm looking up information on." She paused. "The slight problem is that my mother refused to let me bring it with me."

"Your *mother?*"

"She's the head of the Wildwood Coven." Robin studied the cabinet, her lips pressing together. "I caved in to her demands to avoid an argument. Besides, I don't need—"

She broke off as Tansy vanished behind the cabinet, her fluffy tail disappearing from sight.

"Tansy!" Robin took a step closer, only to recoil when Tansy shot out from behind the cabinet with a book clutched in her paws. "I'm pretty sure 'don't touch the door' applied to you as well."

The grating noise sounded again, and the walls began to spin, spikes and all.

"Oh boy." I skimmed down the list of words I'd written in my Biblio-Witch Inventory and tapped the word *stop*.

The room ground to a halt, to my relief, but the knee-high spikes still blocked our path to the door, while others jutted from the walls.

I could only think of one way out. "I think we'll have to fly through."

"You mean on a broomstick?"

"Unless you have one hidden away, I'll have to levitate us out. All of us."

"Don't worry about Tansy. She's so good at jumping she might as well have wings of her own."

"Well... all right." I tapped the word *fly*, and both Robin and I flew upwards, ungracefully soaring over the spikes.

When we landed outside, Tansy squeaked loudly and leapt through the door. It slammed on our heels, and a sound alarmingly similar to a pair of giant teeth snapping followed.

"Hold the door!" I didn't bother with the padlocks, grabbing my Biblio-Witch Inventory instead and hitting the word *lock*. The door re-sealed itself at once, the padlocks snapping back into place.

Robin released a breath, eyeing the book in my hands. "So that's what you meant by manipulating words with magic."

"Yeah. It's useful in situations like this." I grimaced at another thud from behind the door. "Sorry we didn't get the book you needed."

A squeak came from our feet, and we both looked down to where Tansy held up the book in her little hands.

"Nice job, Tansy," Robin said approvingly, taking the book from her familiar. "I hope there's an easier way to return it to its proper place afterwards."

"So do I." I studied the leather-bound cover. "How'd she manage to break into the cabinet?"

"Tansy is good at getting in and out of places," she replied. "Anyway, sorry about the close call. Do you often nearly end up getting impaled when you go looking for rare books?"

"Occasionally, but I should have asked Sylvester to come with us," I said. "He might have at least warned me."

"Did you say he belongs to your entire family?" Robin glanced around as if concerned that he might be listening in again. "He doesn't strike me as a typical familiar. Tansy thinks so too."

She wasn't wrong, and I had a feeling any lie I told wouldn't fool an expert like Robin. I'd never met someone who knew so much about familiars that she recognised Sylvester as something else entirely, and not a regular animal either.

"Sylvester has been here a long time," I evaded. "Since before the library was enchanted. It's a long story, but we still discover new things about the library every day. Sylvester is just one of its mysteries."

"Makes sense." She nodded. "Thanks for the help."

"I hope the book is useful."

"Given that I'm not going back in there anytime soon,

so do I." She tucked the book under her arm and followed me to the stairs. "Ah… whereabouts is the Magical Creatures Division?"

"Third floor," I said. "Why?"

"I thought I might as well check it out since I'm here."

"Sure," I said. "Erm, my cousin is up on the third floor, and she tends to have some weird pets, so if you hear any noises, don't be alarmed."

Her brows shot up. "No mystery monsters?"

"Not to my knowledge, but she's very interested to find out the identity of the creature visiting the beach." I spotted a damp and dishevelled Estelle emerging from a nearby corridor. "I'll catch you up."

"Sure." Robin headed up to the third floor, and I watched for a moment to make sure she didn't accidentally wander into the Dimensional Studies Section. As long as no more mechanical spikes decided to attack her, she could cope without me being there, so I went to join my cousin.

Spark the pixie flew out to catch up with Estelle, who pushed a handful of dripping-wet hair out of her eyes. "I heard crashing noises. Everything okay?"

"I discovered the Artefacts Section, and I think it nearly ate me."

"Oh no," she said. "What were you looking for? It only does that when someone walks in that it doesn't fully trust."

"Ah… a guest from the inn wanted my help researching wands and other artefacts, and when she couldn't open the cabinet, her familiar stole the book she needed instead."

"That would explain it."

"Sorry," I said. "In fairness, the room was full of deadly spikes at the time."

"What did she need?" Estelle asked. "It must have been unusual if the room tried to take a bite out of her."

"Wait, you mean the room itself was actually trying to eat us?"

"It likes people with interesting secrets."

I arched a brow. "Are you *sure* I wasn't the intended target? I'm surprised any of us can get in there."

"Oh, it doesn't harm our family," she said. "It likes secrets from outside the library, which means that whatever secret your guest was keeping isn't connected to us in the slightest."

"I should have figured from the size of the padlocks on the door that it was something like that," I said. "My mistake. Anyway, I'll have to ask what her secret is."

I was starting to wish I'd accompanied Robin up to the third floor anyway, just to protect her from a potential run-in with Cass—though their mutual liking for magical creatures and familiars might be a bonding moment for them. Before I could head upstairs, however, Robin herself came back downstairs with Tansy scurrying along the banisters and caught up to Estelle and me.

"No trouble?" I asked her. "Did you see my cousin?"

"I heard her. She told me not to disturb the beasts."

"Sounds like her." I indicated Estelle. "This is my cousin, Estelle. The nice cousin."

"As opposed to the lost one?"

"You heard that nickname?" The moniker 'Lost Cousin' had been attached to me since before most people in town had even met me, thanks to a dedication in one of

Aunt Candace's books that happened to be based on my dad's life story.

"Someone I ran into at the pet shop used that name."

I suppressed a groan. "I guess you met my aunt."

"She left right after I got there," she replied. "Anyway, can I temporarily check out this book for the week? If I'm allowed, as a tourist."

"Sure." I didn't blame her for not wanting to read it in the library after the room had tried to eat us. "I'll sort it out when we get downstairs."

At the bottom of the stairs, I made my way to the desk and found the owl where I'd left him, pretending to be asleep.

"Thanks for warning me about the room trying to eat us, Sylvester."

"You're welcome." He opened his eyes and faked a yawn. "I take it you escaped alive?"

"I did at least get the book I wanted without losing my fingers." On balance, I decided against mentioning to him that Robin had guessed he wasn't an ordinary owl. He'd seemed to like her, which was a rarity for Sylvester, and I didn't need to put them at odds. Especially if I did end up needing to ask for the Forbidden Room's help uncovering our mystery beast.

"The spikes are made of rubber, did you know?"

"Excuse me?" I studied the owl's face. "Is that true?"

"Obviously," he said. "You should have asked."

"I didn't even know there were spikes at all, let alone rubber ones." I reached for the record book. "Now, please stop sitting on the records."

"Rubber!" said Robin, as I wrestled the book from

underneath Sylvester's clawed feet. "I should have known it was a trick."

Sylvester cackled to himself, while I helped Robin check out the book and handed it over to her. "This is a temporary pass. How long are you staying in town for?"

"Until the weekend. I'll have it back to you before then." She jumped when Sylvester took flight in an abrupt beat of his wings, disappearing among the stacks. "Also... about that mystery monster of yours..."

"You heard about that too?" Estelle approached us, waving her wand to dry out her cloak and hair. "That owl. I'm sure he knows we figured out he's the one who dropped that mouse down the sink upstairs."

"Probably," I said. "What about the monster, Robin?"

"I'd like to have a closer look at the scene of the attack," she said. "Like I said, I have an affinity with animals, and Tansy is good at identifying creatures by scent. The police were blocking the way earlier, I know, but I figured you might be able to convince them to let me sneak a look."

"Are you sure?" I asked. "I mean—I'd have assumed you'd ask Cass, not me."

"She strikes me as a loner."

"You aren't wrong. Estelle, can you watch the desk for a bit? I know this isn't really library-related..."

"It is," she said. "If Cass *and* Aunt Candace are likely to get into trouble over this mysterious beast, then the sooner we deal with it, the better."

I couldn't have agreed more. "I'll be back soon."

6

After leaving the library, Robin and I walked across the square to the beach. Tansy ran ahead, her bright tail flickering in the sunlight as she happily chased seagulls across the waterfront.

"I bet you had no trouble practising using signals to identify your familiar in a crowd," I remarked to Robin. "Jet is a chatterbox, but crows aren't as distinctive as bright-red squirrels."

"Tansy does like to stand out."

We followed her bright-red tail to the pier, which had been vacated, though several tourists had gathered on the beach. It was a nice day, so I didn't blame them for wanting to enjoy the sunshine despite the ominous air hanging around the pier. When the last seagull took flight, Tansy scampered over to the pier and began to sniff around the rope barrier.

"The salt water might make it tricky for her to pick up the creature's scent," Robin told me. "And the fact that there have been people all over the place all day. Worth a shot, though."

"Agreed." At least certain family members of mine weren't around, though I kept an eye out for them while Tansy explored the pier.

"You're staying at the hotel near the seafront?" I asked Robin. "I'm surprised nobody there heard the creature making a racket last night. There's no quiet way to rip up a bunch of wooden beams."

"We're not that close to the pier, though," she said. "I didn't hear anything, but I slept with earplugs in anyway—what is it, Tansy?"

Tansy returned to Robin's side and communicated with her in squeaks while Robin listened intently.

"What did she say?" I asked her when Tansy had finished "speaking."

She sucked in a breath. "Tansy is pretty certain that a human was here at the same time as the creature was."

"A human?" I asked. "Are you sure they weren't in the crowd earlier?"

"No, she thinks they were standing on the broken part of the pier, close to the end. They didn't let the crowd get that close."

"If they were, then where'd they go?" Even if they'd been attacked by the creature, there would have been traces left behind. "Can Tansy identify the creature?"

Robin shook her head. "The saltwater smell is too strong, and it's an unfamiliar scent to her. But she said there was definitely a person out there... and some other kind of animal."

"Another animal?" What on earth had happened here last night?

"Her theory is that a shifter came here," said Robin.

"A shifter." *Oh.* Was there some truth in the joke I'd made about aquatic werewolves after all? "A shifter couldn't have ripped up the pier like that, right?"

Robin shook her head. "Without witnesses, it's impossible to say."

"There were witnesses the night before, allegedly, but they were drunk at the time." It might be worth speaking to them after all, if just to clarify whether they'd accidentally mistaken a shifter for a dangerous mystery monster. "What's your theory?"

Her gaze travelled over the pier. "Honestly, it doesn't look like there was any kind of a struggle. The damage to the pier looks more like the creature accidentally fell through or tore up the wooden beams trying to get out of the water."

"Must have been heavy, then. Like one of Edwin's troll guards, but I'm not sure they can swim."

"I doubt it was one of them," she said. "They tend to be aware of their own strength. Another explanation is that the damage was inflicted deliberately."

"Why? To cover up what really went on here?"

"That or to make it look as if a monster came to the beach," she said. "Tansy thinks so, anyway."

"Why would anyone do that?" And just what had happened to the bait Cass had left out, if this was a setup? "I thought... well, the witch from the pet shop says people keep asking her whether someone has picked a particularly weird choice of a familiar."

"I doubt it," said Robin. "I know familiars. They stick close to their witch or wizard. Might be a pet, given the proximity to humans, but a shifter is more likely."

"Whatever it is, they must be as confident on the land as they are in the water."

Robin's gaze landed on a spot behind me. "Oh great. I should have guessed he'd come looking for me."

I turned, seeing her brother approaching us from the direction of the inn. He did indeed have a hedgehog sitting on his shoulder, which might have been adorable if both of them hadn't been wearing expressions that rivalled Cass's when someone disturbed her while she was with her animals.

"You'd better go," Robin advised me. "I'm going to refrain from mentioning the room that tried to eat us. He'd probably try to have you arrested for attempted murder."

"That wouldn't work out." I *hoped* not, anyway. "I should head back to the library to give Estelle a hand."

"If your books make a habit of attacking you, then she probably needs the help." She grinned. "I didn't expect this much excitement from a small town by the beach."

"Glad we could entertain you," I said wryly. "I hope the book is useful too."

As I turned away, I could hear Robin and Tansy talking to one another, but I couldn't make out any words as the former kept her voice down and the latter was mostly squeaking. I wondered whether Robin had been entirely forthcoming with what her familiar had found at the site of the creature's appearance, though she'd given me far more information than I could ever have worked out for myself. *A shifter, though?* Or if not, a setup? Who would want to fake a monster attack?

There was also the fact that she'd come close to figuring out that Sylvester wasn't a normal owl, but I'd be the one who ended up getting hit by the backlash if he found out, so I'd hold my tongue.

Upon returning to the library, I found Estelle dealing with yet more students asking for help finding books for their last-minute study efforts.

"No, I don't have a book that will magically make you able to recall information you haven't actually read about," she was telling a group of teens who'd gathered around the desk. "I can't magic up a substitute for doing the work. Not one that won't get you kicked out of the academy, anyway."

Grumbling complaints ensued as their group sloped away, no doubt to whine about the unfairness of having to study for exams. I sidestepped them, and they left the library through the front door.

"Having fun?" I crossed to the desk.

"They're ridiculous," Estelle said. "Absolutely no work ethic whatsoever. I think they'd have tried to convince me to take the exam for them if they could have got away with it."

"You wouldn't have actually said yes?"

"Of course not." She snorted. "They can barely cast basic spells, and it sounds like they've spent all their free time throwing parties on the beach instead of practising."

"Wait, they were the ones who saw the monster?" It was no wonder they hadn't been studying, and while they clearly weren't the most reliable witnesses, they were all we had. I could suffer through a conversation with them to get a clue or two, right?

Estelle eyed the door. "You're not going to help them, are you?"

"I'm going to ask about the mystery monster." I opened

the door and emerged behind the group of students, letting it close behind me before addressing them. "Hey. Excuse me?"

"What?" The girl who answered was sullen-looking and raven-haired, and I recognised her as the owner of the speaker I'd turned off a couple of days ago. I cast my mind around for the name the other students had used. Marla Hutchins. "Your sister threw us out."

"She's my cousin, and you were asking her to break the academy's rules. She's a trainee lecturer. You can hardly ask her to help you cheat."

"What's it to you?" Marla said. "My mum's on the school board, you know. I can ask her to give me an exemption if I tell her the librarians refused to help me."

That was uncalled for. "Does she know you've been throwing parties on the beach and in the library instead of studying?"

I hadn't expected it to be easy to get through to her, but it was no wonder even Aunt Candace had given up trying to question her. What might change her mind?

Marla turned away in disgust. "I hate people like you."

I bit back a sarcastic response. "People who do the work, you mean? Maybe I can help you study."

"Yeah, right."

"I can help." An idea struck me. "But only if you do something for me first."

"Like what?"

"Tell me about the monster you saw at the beach the other day." I addressed her friends as well as Marla. "If you describe it to my satisfaction, I'll help you prepare for your exam."

MONSTERS & MANUSCRIPTS

"Describe it?" Her forehead scrunched up. "I dunno. It was big."

"I gathered. Bigger than a person?"

"Massive. Yeah. Hairy too."

"Hairy?" I repeated. "It wasn't a shifter, was it?"

"No, too big." She shuddered. "It had massive claws too."

"What about teeth?"

"Big ones, yeah," she said. "That enough?"

"Where did you see it, exactly?" I asked. "Did it come out of the water? On the pier?"

"Nah, it was under the pier. Eating something."

Cass's bait. I should have known.

"You said you'd help us," added one of her friends. "We've told you what we know. Now tell us how to pass the exam."

"That's right," said Marla. "Go on, pay up."

"Tell me what your exam is about first."

"It's a practical exam."

Perfect. "There's a room up on the library's second floor that should be able to help you. I'll get the key."

She shot me a suspicious look, but I put on a smile and pushed open the door to the library again. Estelle raised her brows when the students entered behind me, while I reached for the key I'd left on the desk and handed it to Marla Hutchins.

"Take this and unlock the door," I told her. "The room has our best books on practical magic in the entire library. Jet will take you there."

The little crow came swooping over to me. "Here, partner!"

"Can you escort these students up to the second floor,

to the Magical Artefacts Division?" I spoke in a low voice. "It's behind a door with two massive padlocks on it. Do that and I'll give you a treat."

He cawed with enthusiasm when I produced the bag of treats. "Yes, partner!"

"Let me know when you're done," I told the students. "Best of luck."

Estelle watched them leave. "What was that about?"

"I told them they can find help with their practical exam up in the Artefacts Division," I explained. "Not a lie. At best they'll be out of our hair for a bit, and at worst, they'll get a good scare from those fake spikes."

She laughed. "What gave you that idea?"

"They wanted my help for tomorrow's exam, and *I* wanted them to tell me what the mystery monster looked like. So we did a trade."

"That was... devious."

"I think Cass might be rubbing off on me," I admitted. "I wasn't going to help them cheat, though, and the information they gave me wasn't exactly specific."

I grabbed my notepad and pen and set about drawing the students' description of the mystery monster to show to Estelle. Neither of us could figure out what the features belonged to, but it kept us entertained for a bit.

When the students came downstairs, shell-shocked and with their hair standing on end, we both feigned shock and surprise.

"Is everyone all right?" I asked.

"Barely," said Marla accusingly. "You could have killed us."

"The room's harmless," I told them. "The spikes are made of rubber."

"*What?*" said Marla. "I'll tell my mum. I will."

"You'll do no such thing." Sylvester appeared and released a deafening hoot.

The students took one look at the giant owl and fled, through the door and out into the square.

I watched the door swing shut behind them in bewilderment. "Er, thanks, Sylvester. Were you watching the whole time?"

"Obviously," he said. "That *was* devious of you, Aurora. You and the vampire have more in common than I ever thought."

"You can't seriously compare me to Evangeline." I scowled at him. "You're the one I got the idea from."

To my utter consternation, Sylvester stole a treat from the bag on the desk and took flight, cackling the whole time. *That owl.*

Dinner that evening was notable only because everyone was present for once—a rarity. I often went out with Xavier in the evening, or Estelle went on dates, or Cass asked for her food to be brought up to the third floor and refused to come down, or Aunt Candace did the same when she was in her study and on a book deadline. Today, though, everyone sat down to platefuls of bangers and mash. Aunt Adelaide gave her sister a disapproving stare when she shovelled half a plateful of mashed potatoes in her mouth at once.

"Don't be disgusting, Candace," said Aunt Adelaide.

Aunt Candace made an indistinct noise, swallowed, and said, "I was paying you a compliment."

"I hope you've had a productive day, Candace," said Aunt Adelaide. "I also hope you didn't cause poor Edwin too much trouble with your questioning."

Aunt Candace scoffed. "He was clueless before I showed up. If anything, I was a great help to him. I even identified some creatures that might fit the profile of this mystery beast."

Oh no. She hadn't just been researching for a book. She'd also been attempting to "help" Edwin. Or take over the investigation. Either way, my sympathy for him increased considerably.

Cass scoffed. "You probably listed a bunch of creatures that don't actually exist. Like Bigfoot."

"Doesn't exist?" Aunt Candace put on a wounded expression. "Honestly, Cass. You're taking a cheap shot at an already vulnerable creature. I expected better of you."

Cass looked unimpressed. "If he does exist, he's hardly going to be swimming in the sea in the south of England, is he?"

I choked on a laugh. "I don't think it was Bigfoot, but I'm not convinced it came from the water either. The students said it had fur or hair, not scales."

"You asked the students?" Aunt Adelaide raised a brow.

I pulled out the drawing I'd sketched out earlier when I'd been trying to represent their description on paper. "They said it had claws or massive paws, big feet, fur, teeth…"

"Wings?" asked Cass.

"I never asked. It wouldn't be in the water if it had wings, I assumed." I showed the others my notepad. "Does that look like any creatures you're familiar with?"

"No, it looks like a blob," Cass commented.

Honestly. "I never claimed to be an artist, you know."

"I thought it was a self-portrait," put in Aunt Candace.

I rolled my eyes. "You know of all kinds of weird monsters. Surely you can think of at least one who fits the description."

"Like I said." Aunt Candace picked up her fork again. "Bigfoot."

I could imagine just how thrilled the police had been with her "help." "Robin and her familiar had a look around, and she claimed that a human might have been near the spot where the creature appeared. At the same time. That might mean it's tame."

"You think it was someone's pet?" asked Estelle. "Or wild animal friend?"

"Or shifter?" Aunt Adelaide ventured.

"That's what Robin suggested, but the students insisted whatever they saw was way bigger than the average shifter," I explained. "That doesn't mean there wasn't one in the area, though." If anyone would pick up on the scent of a strange creature in town, it was the shifters.

"Maybe it's a rogue." Aunt Candace sounded intrigued. "The pack might be trying to bring a runaway shifter under control without involving the police. They tend to be territorial and like keeping matters within the pack alone, so it makes sense for them to have kept it quiet."

That sounded far more plausible than the 'Bigfoot' theory, though I hadn't had many interactions with the pack myself. We did have a few regular werewolf visitors at the library, though they seemed to prefer raiding the free buffet to studying or picking up any of our books. Regardless, I probably shouldn't have put too much stock in Aunt Candace's theories, considering they came from the perspective of someone more interested in getting a good story than anything else.

"A rogue is unlikely," Aunt Adelaide put in. "If it's a werewolf, a rogue would be more likely to be roaming around the countryside than the beach."

"Shark shifter?" Aunt Candace asked. "Whale shifter? Dolphin?"

"You're just naming random animals now," said Aunt Adelaide.

"You can't be completely incurious about this beast." Aunt Candace's gaze skimmed over all of us. "Even you, Cass?"

"Keep me out of this." My cousin put down her fork. "I've had enough of this nonsense."

"Cass, you aren't still leaving bait out for the creature, are you?" I knew the question wouldn't win me her support, but given what I'd heard from the students, it was a safe bet that her gesture hadn't gone unnoticed.

Cass gave me a withering look. "If I am, there's exactly nothing you can do to stop me. Nor your new friend either."

I shook my head at her. "If you mean Robin, then she's more likely to try leaving bait out herself, not stop you."

"Am I supposed to know who Robin is?" asked Aunt Candace.

"She's a guest at the inn," I explained. "She has a red squirrel familiar, so you must have seen her around the beach."

"Was she in the library too?"

"Yes, she was." I shifted in my seat when everyone turned towards me, but if it stopped Cass from storming off, then I'd share whatever I could. "Robin and I also had a look around the pier, which is where her familiar claimed to have picked up a shifter's scent near the spot where the creature appeared. The two of them can communicate with one another the same way we can with Jet and Sylvester."

"The Wildwoods," said Aunt Adelaide. "I knew the name sounded familiar."

"You know her?" I asked.

"I know of her family," said my aunt. "They're widely regarded in their region, powerful and respected. As far as I know, there's at least one Head Witch in their family too."

A Head Witch, I recalled, was a representative who stood for all the witches and wizards of that particular region of the UK. Due to their power and prestige, the Head Witches were usually also coven leaders.

"She can communicate with animals," I said to her. "The whole family can. That's their gift."

"Interesting," said Aunt Candace. "Yes, I researched them. They have quite the media profile. So that's why they know about magical beasts... I wonder whether it's a coincidence that they showed up when they did."

"I wondered the same," I admitted, "but they weren't looking up anything about mythical beasts when they came to the library."

Regardless of whether the Wildwoods' arrival in town was coincidental or not, Robin's comments about shifters might be worth looking into. If one of them had interacted with the creature, then finding out who it was might be our key to identifying the mystery beast. Preferably before it struck again.

7

The following day, I woke from a dead sleep when a feathery wing brushed against my nose, making me sneeze. My eyes cracked open to the alarming sight of Sylvester perched on my bedside table, looming over my face.

"What was that in aid of?" I swatted the owl away with my hand. "Shoo."

He shuffled back haughtily. "It might interest you to know that your mystery monster has attacked someone else."

Attacked someone?

Instantly awake, I jumped out of bed and ran downstairs, where I found a sleepy Estelle and Aunt Adelaide on the sofa in the living room. Sylvester came swooping in after me.

"Woke you, too, did he?" Estelle yawned. "I don't know what this is about either, for the record."

Footsteps thundered, and Aunt Candace came flying

downstairs at such speed that it was a wonder she didn't fall on her face. "I missed it again!"

"What actually happened?" I looked up when Sylvester landed on top of a nearby cabinet. "Nobody got hurt, right?"

"I don't know, do I?" said Aunt Candace.

"You aren't the one I was asking." I watched Sylvester in the hopes that he'd enlighten us all. "Since when did you pay attention to the latest gossip, anyway?"

"I thought it was in all our interests for me to keep an eye on current events," said the owl. "Especially those of us who insist upon getting involved."

"Don't look at me. I didn't spend the entire morning questioning the police yesterday or leave out bait for the creature." I glanced towards the stairs. "Where's Cass, anyway?"

"She told me to go away when I knocked on her door," Estelle answered.

"At least she isn't at the beach, then."

"That's what worried me," said Aunt Adelaide. "I could have sworn I heard her go out last night. I might have been mistaken, though."

"She didn't, did she?" I hoped she wouldn't go back so soon, but I'd known trying to talk her out of her pursuit of the monster at dinner was a futile endeavour. None of us could stand between Cass and her attempt to befriend every magical creature that crossed her path.

"I thought I heard someone go out, too, but I assumed it was Laney," said Estelle. "Though vampires usually don't make any noise, thinking about it."

"I'll check on Laney," I offered. "In case she saw Cass go out."

I went upstairs to the first floor and headed down the corridor to the guest room she'd claimed. As expected, I didn't hear any sound from behind the door, but vampires slept like the dead, excuse the pun. It wasn't usually wise to disturb a sleeping vampire—in fact, even Sylvester left her alone—but Laney was my best friend, so I was reasonably confident she wouldn't attack me while half-asleep. I nudged open the door and whispered, "Laney?"

In the single bed in the corner, Laney stirred and then shielded her eyes against the light streaming through a gap in the curtains. "Hmm? Rory? What is it?"

"Sorry I woke you," I said. "Apparently, the mystery monster appeared and attacked someone last night. Did you know?"

She squinted at me blearily. "First I've heard."

"Same, but I was just checking to make sure nobody here was around at the time," I explained. "Ah—did you see Cass go out last night?"

"Nope." She yawned, her jaw cracking. "Not that I was looking at her. Why, is she up to her usual mischief?"

"I'll find out," I said. "Once Sylvester deigns to tell us what went on out there. Wish me luck."

"Good luck." She flopped back on her pillows and was out like a light.

After closing the door, I stopped off at my room to properly get dressed. Once I'd put my cloak on, I went back downstairs to the living room, where Aunt Adelaide and Estelle were still trying to pry the details of last night's events out of Sylvester.

"I wasn't there," he insisted. "Ask that familiar of yours."

"You mean *my* familiar?" I swivelled around to Aunt Candace. "What did you do, send Jet out to spy for you?"

"As if I could stop him if I wanted to," she scoffed. "Why does it matter?"

"We have to sit an exam next week," I told her. "No wonder he can't stay awake through our study sessions if you have him flying out at all hours of the night."

"She's right there," Estelle said. "Why not get your own familiar?"

"I haven't the time to take care of a familiar."

"But plenty of time to hassle the police?" I left before she could reply, heading into the lobby to look for my familiar. "Jet?"

The little crow descended in a flutter of black wings. "Yes, partner?"

"Jet, what happened at the beach last night?" I asked. "Sylvester said you told him that someone was attacked. Did you see?"

"No, but everyone on the beach was talking about it!" His wings flapped in agitation. "People staying at the inn were kept awake all night!"

"By what?"

"Screaming, growling, all kinds of noises." He screeched in demonstration, causing me to cover my ears.

"No need for that," I told him. "Do you mean human screaming? Or something else?"

A loud thud came from behind me as Aunt Candace flew upstairs with speed that rivalled a vampire, without waiting to hear the rest.

"I guess she wants to be where the action is," I remarked. "Jet, you don't have to go outside when she asks you to. I need you to be focused on our exam, okay?"

"But partner, what if someone was hurt?"

"That's for the police to find out," I said firmly. "Not Aunt Candace. We'll check with the others, okay?"

Aunt Adelaide and Estelle appeared to have given up trying to wrangle answers out of Sylvester and had made for the kitchen instead. When I crossed the living room, Aunt Candace came rattling back downstairs and made straight for the lobby. At least she was wearing clothes this time, though the notebook in her hand gave away her intentions.

"You're going to pester Edwin at a time like this?" I called after her.

"Obviously," she said. "I want the details."

"Didn't Jet already give them to you?"

"Unidentified noises in the dead of night are not enough to make a good story."

"I'm sure Edwin would disagree." I looked to Sylvester, who remained perched on top of the cabinet, and then to Jet. "Also, you're not taking my familiar with you unless I come too. Jet, stay put."

He landed on the arm of the sofa, his beady eyes following Aunt Candace's retreat. When the library's front door slammed behind her, I rolled my eyes. "Does she honestly think the police would rather talk to her than the actual witnesses?"

"No doubt." Aunt Adelaide leaned out of the kitchen doorway, wearing a disgruntled expression. "If you want to follow her, please try to make it back before opening time. And tell me everything."

"I will." I left the living quarters, and Estelle caught up to me in the lobby.

"I'm coming too," she said. "It might need two of us to wrangle Aunt Candace."

"You aren't wrong." I beckoned to Jet, and we made our way to the front door.

When we got outside, Aunt Candace was already halfway across the square. I pitied whoever had to answer her questions this time around, but my primary concern was making sure that our family didn't end up getting blamed. If Cass *had* slipped out of the library at night and had been spotted, then there wouldn't be much any of us could do to prevent her from taking the hit.

I didn't always get on with my cousin, but her heart was in the right place as far as magical creatures were concerned. Would that hold up if it turned out the creature had attacked someone, though?

Estelle and I passed by the clock tower and reached the seafront. The beach was mostly deserted, but raised voices echoed from the direction of the police station. At least a dozen people queued up by the automatic doors, talking over one another and forming a barricade. Aunt Candace stood on tiptoe at the back of the line, trying to see inside the station.

"I can fly into the station and listen for clues, partner!" Jet squeaked.

"Sure, why not."

The little crow would find it easier to get past the crowd than the rest of us since the doors were open for anyone to walk in. Anyone who could get through the crowd, anyway, which did not include Aunt Candace despite her best efforts to elbow people aside. Her notebook hovered next to her, pen scribbling away, but it was beyond me to figure out what she was taking note of.

People she intended to kill off in her next book for getting in the way of her attempts to find out the gossip, perhaps.

Estelle and I waited outside, trying to listen to snatches of conversation without much luck.

A few minutes passed before Jet flew back to my side. "Partner, nobody saw the creature, but the people staying at the inn heard screaming and growling coming from down on the beach!"

"That's what you already heard, right?" Had nothing new arisen? It was better than hearing of a genuine attack, of course, but you'd think someone would have looked out the window for the source of the noise.

"From which part of the beach?" Aunt Candace watched Jet, her notebook and pen bobbing at her side. "Show me."

"He doesn't know," I told her. "It might not even have been the inn, given how sounds echo at night."

I gave the crowd a scan, but Robin and her family didn't appear to be in it. I would have recognised Tansy's bright-red tail anywhere.

Aunt Candace tutted. "I'll play detective myself, then."

She tramped down the walkway, notebook hovering at her side, and Estelle and I hastened to follow her in case she barged into the inn and started hassling the guests. Aunt Candace halted behind the pier, though, and squinted at the ruined planks. "Looks the same as yesterday. If I had to guess, the creature came out of the water elsewhere."

"The tide was in," said Estelle. "If the beast left footprints, they'll have been washed away."

Undeterred, Aunt Candace walked away from the pier and climbed down from the walkway to the beach.

I beckoned to my familiar. "Jet, who exactly claimed to have heard the screaming?"

"The guests at the inn!" he squeaked.

If the sound had been audible to everyone, then Robin must have heard, even if she'd been wearing earplugs as she'd claimed the previous day. Leaving Aunt Candace to wander up and down the sand, Estelle and I crossed the walkway until we came to the inn that stood on the road connecting the seafront to the town square. One wall faced the beach, overlooking the sand, and I scanned the surrounding area.

Estelle peered up and down the beach. "I don't see anything out of place."

"Except Aunt Candace." She ran up and down the sound, a spring in her step as if she was on her way to Disneyland. "Has she seen something, do you think?"

We made our way down to the sand again, joining her near the ruin of an old tree that had been stripped to the bone by the elements. Aunt Candace beamed and pointed to the edge of the tree, which was marked as if a set of claws had raked along its bark.

"No signs of a struggle," she mused. "But that is most definitely a *clue*."

"If you say so." I scanned the ruined tree, which must have washed up from elsewhere. "It's been here for ages, though, and that claw mark might have come from anything."

"This is new." Estelle crouched and indicated a grey mass caught between the branches of the tree. "Is that... fur?"

Aunt Candace reached out a hand, snagging a tangle of

what appeared to be thick grey fur. "You'd make a fine detective yourself, Estelle."

"That," I said, "is werewolf fur. Even I know that."

Aunt Candace shot me a scowl. "Doesn't mean it isn't a clue."

It might be. Robin and Tansy had said there might have been shifters around the pier the previous day. If it *was* a shifter behind the "attacks," then Cass would rapidly lose interest—but Aunt Candace would be less likely to give up her quest for a good story regardless of the outcome. To find out whether any shifters had been at the beach, we'd need to speak to a member of the pack, though, and I hadn't seen any of them at the police station.

"Yes, it is." Aunt Candace bounded along the beach, heading for the police station. "I'll make sure they know what I found. I'm sure they'll be grateful."

"I don't think Edwin will buy it," I said to Estelle in an undertone. "There are no traces of... of blood or anything that indicates someone was attacked. The screaming *might* have been a werewolf instead."

"Your guess is as good as mine," Estelle said. "I think we should head back to the library."

"Yeah." I gave the claw marks another scan. "Out of curiosity, how might I go about talking to the pack? Is there a shifter representative, like with the vampires?"

On second thought, maybe I didn't want to be the one to tell the shifter equivalent of Evangeline that one of the local shifters might be running amok and attacking people on the beach. If the shifters' leader was anything like the head vampire, that would end badly for all of us.

"There is," answered Estelle. "He's a werewolf—shifter

pack leaders usually are—and he lives way out on the edge of town. Chief Tarquin, he's called."

"Do you think he'd be willing to talk to us?" I asked. "If a shifter was at the beach at the same time as the mystery monster, they count as a witness, even if they were running around in animal form."

"Maybe." Worry flickered across her features. "Chief Tarquin is reasonable enough, but I don't know that he'd take well to accusations of one of his shifters running around the beach attacking people."

"That might not be what happened here, though. In fact, I'm almost certain it wasn't."

She blew out a breath. "Still risky. Shifters can be…"

"Temperamental? You're forgetting I live in the same building as Cass."

"True." Estelle gave me a faint smile. "Just, you know. Vampires and werewolves are notorious rivals, even here."

"Oh." While the vampires of Ivory Beach seemed to dislike the Reapers above all else, that didn't mean they wouldn't notice if I tried talking to the shifters. And the shifters themselves might not be willing to talk to me if they knew I had a vampire for a best friend. "If one of them witnessed the attack, though? They haven't come forward yet, and I gather that they prefer to keep shifter-related business within the pack anyway."

"Yes. I mean, it could be a rogue," she allowed. "The Chief likes to keep that sort of thing quiet, but Edwin would want to know. I'm not sure it's even occurred to him to ask the shifters yet."

"He's dealing with half the inn's guests complaining, by the looks of things," I said. "Not to mention Aunt Candace is waiting to pounce on the first person to leave the station. I doubt the shifters want *her* to be the first member of our family they meet up with, especially if she waves that werewolf fur in their faces."

"You make a valid point," said Estelle. "I don't know that you should go alone, though, but one of us definitely needs to go back to the library in case Sylvester causes another flood or Cass tries to give us the slip to go looking for monsters."

"I can take Jet with me." I beckoned to the little crow. "It'll stop Aunt Candace from sending him fishing for gossip when we're supposed to be practising for the exam too."

"Finding your way to the pack's home as a team would be a good training exercise," said Estelle. "Learning outside of a classroom might be better for both of you."

"Good idea," I said. "Can you give Jet the shifters' address? If he leads us to the right place without having to consult me, I can give him a reward. Does that sound good, Jet?"

"Yes, partner!" He perched on Estelle's hand as she told him the directions to the shifters' part of town and the chief's address while I refrained from listening in. I could always text Estelle if he forgot.

"Good luck," Estelle said. "Just… don't go past the vampires' territory. I don't think any of them will be awake at this time, but Evangeline isn't likely to be thrilled if she learns where you're going."

"I figured." I owed Evangeline a favour that she hadn't called me back for yet, and which I had zero intention of mentioning in front of the chief. Still, no part of our agreement said that I couldn't *talk* to the shifters, and if they knew anything about this mystery monster, I needed to ask before my aunt got there first.

Estelle and I parted ways, and Jet flew ahead of me towards the shifters' part of town. This was certainly one way to test our skills as a witch-and-familiar team, and for all I knew, being around a bunch of scary people who could shift into animals might be just the incentive he needed to pay attention to my instructions. Better than being stuck in a classroom, at any rate.

Thanks to our need to avoid the vampires' home, we had to walk on a twisting route and Jet got left and right mixed up a few times, but we made it to the shifters' part of town within half an hour. The shifters' homes were spread out with plenty of fields and parks in between to provide ample space for them to run around in animal form.

With Jet's guidance, I found the right street and knocked on the door to a whitewashed house with wide, open windows. The modern cars parked in the drive and the wide lawns were the polar opposite to the vampires' gloomy church with its oppressive atmosphere. A youngish man with sandy hair and a surfer's physique answered the door—I noticed the latter because he wasn't wearing a shirt. Shifters tended to have different standards for modesty than the rest of us, mostly because they tended to lose all their clothes when they shifted into animal form. At least he was wearing shorts.

"Hi," I said awkwardly. "Are you Chief Tarquin?"

"No, he's my dad," he replied. "I'm Patch. You're one of the library witches, aren't you?"

"Yes. I'm Rory. I moved here a few months ago."

"Oh, you're the lost cousin."

Even the werewolves had heard that nickname? "I've been called that. Is your dad around?"

"Sure, come on in."

Whatever I'd expected, it wasn't an instant invitation into the house. While part of me remained sure that the pack must have heard about my family's entanglement with the vampires, his smile was friendly enough, so I followed him into a wide, airy conservatory. A surfboard stood against the nearby wall next to a pair of flip-flops.

"Ah—do you go to the beach a lot, by any chance?" I asked him.

"Sure," he replied. "Why?"

"Were you there yesterday?" When he raised a brow, I went on. "You might have heard about an incident at the beach last night."

His friendly expression vanished. "I'm not sure I know what incident you're referring to."

I couldn't tell whether he was feigning ignorance or whether he genuinely hadn't heard the latest news. Until I saw him shift, I wouldn't know if he or any of his family members had the dark grey fur Aunt Candace had found on the beach, after all.

"There's been a few incidents in the past few days," I said carefully. "Involving some kind of unknown creature at the beach."

"I don't typically go surfing at night," he said. "So no, I haven't seen anything. I did hear the stories, though. Why, did it appear again last night?"

Was he telling the truth? His wary expression remained intact as if he didn't trust me. Which was fair enough, given that we'd never met before, but how could I possibly explain that Robin's familiar had picked up a shifter's scent without sounding as if I was going out of my way to accuse him?

"Some people staying at the inn heard disturbing noises last night," I explained. "Screaming and growling, according to the reports."

He rolled his eyes. "And when you think of growling, everyone's minds immediately jump to werewolves. Right?"

So he'd already picked up on the direction of my thoughts. "They also found werewolf fur at the beach. The police did." If Aunt Candace had already shown them her discovery, that was technically true, but I opted not to mention my own family members' involvement.

"There's werewolf fur all over the town because we shed like mad in summer," Patch said defensively. "If nobody saw this creature, how can they be sure?"

"A group of students did see the creature," I said. "They described it as being large and covered in hair, and there aren't that many animals who live in the ocean who also fit that description."

"Students?" His brow furrowed. "I don't know what they saw, but it wasn't one of us."

"They were drunk at the time," I allowed. "But it's the only description we have to go by. Last night, there weren't any witnesses, only people who heard screaming. Is shifting typically painful for you?"

"No," he replied. "Some have trouble with their first shift, but generally it's as easy as breathing."

I cast around for a diplomatic way of asking my next question. "What do you normally do if there's a rogue in the area?"

He met my gaze with an animal glint in his eyes that

made me want to take a step back. "Send an emissary to meet with them and try to convince them to either leave or join the local pack. Rogues can be dangerous to the population, so we wouldn't allow one to wander unchecked for days."

"Ah, okay. I'm still new to the magical world, so I wondered how it worked."

"I don't mind answering questions," he said. "I don't know if you've ever seen a werewolf shift, but we're not *that* big, and I don't know that there are many types of shifters that are any larger, if any at all."

"I know," I said. "I'm not making an accusation. I just wanted to hear from a shifter because the only witnesses so far have been humans. You have enhanced senses, don't you? Could you track it by scent?"

"Not in the water," he said. "Some of us are great swimmers, but we can drown as easily as humans can. Anyway, why did you take an interest? You're not with the police."

"No, but I work at the library, and my aunt is researching the incidents for a book." When his expression gained a hint of scepticism again, I added, "There's also my cousin. She's interested in magical creatures."

"You mean Cass." A hint of annoyance entered his voice. "The unpleasant one who likes animals."

"She's... er, she's not that bad once you get to know her." I didn't sound very convincing even to myself, but the problem with Cass was that she downright refused to get to know most people. It sounded as if he was acquainted with her already, though.

"She is," he insisted. "I should know because she dumped my brother last year."

"Really?"

"Yeah, they were together for almost nine months. Then she blew him off."

First Alice at the familiar shop, now the son of the werewolf pack leader? "I only moved to town at the end of the year, so I didn't know."

"Well, I wouldn't mention her name in front of my brother," he said, with the hint of a growl in his voice. "Or my dad."

So much for talking to the pack leader, though it didn't sound as if he knew any more than his sons did. "I won't. She's interested in this creature, but I doubt she'll want to ask questions of the pack."

"I'd think she has more sense." He glanced over his shoulder. "Anyway, like I said, we don't know anything about this beast. If there is one."

"All right." I'd reached the end of my list of questions, and given the way Jet was circling the ceiling, he'd begun to get bored. "I should go back to the library."

"Sure." He walked me to the door. "If you have any more questions, then you can drop by. My dad is usually open to discussing the pack, but we'd know if a shifter was responsible for whatever's going on at the beach."

"Thanks for the help."

I beckoned to Jet to follow me as I left the house and walked down the drive.

"That went better than I thought," I remarked to my familiar. "I was sure that the werewolves would object to me being friends with a vampire, but maybe they don't know about Laney after all."

Not to mention the favour I owed Evangeline, though she might not have wanted word to spread about that either. I doubted she regularly met with the pack chief over brunch.

As for the mystery monster? I was pretty sure Patch had been honest about a shifter not being responsible for the attacks, but that didn't mean the werewolves were entirely ignorant of the creature's true nature. I didn't want to push any further without proof, though. They might not be as secretive as the vampires were, but they wanted to protect their own, which meant keeping their secrets close.

In the meantime, it was time to head back to the library... and have a word with Cass.

8

When I entered the library's lower floor, Estelle had already filled in Aunt Adelaide on everything that had happened on our trip to the beach.

"There you are." Aunt Adelaide waved me over. "What's all this about you going to speak to the shifters' leader? Alone?"

"I took Jet with me, and it went fine," I reassured her.

Her brows rose. "You spoke to the chief?"

"No, his son," I clarified. "Patch. He answered all my questions without an issue. He likes surfing at the beach, so he knows the area pretty well, but he doesn't go there at night, so he didn't witness any of the attacks. He said that the students' description didn't match any shifters since werewolves aren't that big when they shift."

"True, but they could certainly cause the kind of damage we saw on the pier," said Estelle. "Did you mention the fur Aunt Candace found?"

"He said werewolves shed their fur all the time in

summer," I said. "When I asked about rogues, he was pretty adamant that his dad took his job seriously and wouldn't let a rogue wander around the beach for days."

"Makes sense," she said. "The pack has to be careful about that kind of thing, not just because of the secrecy laws, but because if they don't act against rogues, then the vampires will strike instead, which has a tendency to get ugly fast."

"I bet." Evangeline reacted just as swiftly against vampire rogues as well, and I could imagine that they'd show no mercy to any werewolf or other shifter who stepped out of line and didn't have the rest of the pack behind them.

It briefly occurred to me that a vampire would have had the strength to tear up the pier with ease, but vampires didn't have fur *or* claws, so that idea was out. They didn't go near the water if they could help it either. No, it was time for me to think of a new plan towards answers.

"Is Cass still in her room?" I asked.

"No, I think she went up to the third floor," Aunt Adelaide told me. "Without answering any of my questions, I might add."

"She didn't admit to being at the beach last night?"

"Are you surprised?" Estelle asked. "Because I'm not."

"Did *you* know she dated the werewolf chief's son last year?"

"Oh." A grimace tugged at her mouth. "Yeah. That's who she'd recently broken up with when you met her. She was going through a phase of setting Sylvester on anyone who mentioned his name, so I figured I should warn you at the time."

"What about Alice?" I asked, curious.

Her forehead scrunched up. "What about her?"

"She told me that she dated Cass too."

She blinked. "Oh yeah. That was years ago, and I don't know that either of them was particularly committed. How'd that come up?"

"I mentioned Cass's interest in the mystery beast when I dropped into the familiar shop," I explained. "Anyway, I was just curious, considering I ran into two of her exes in the space of a week. I was starting to think Edwin would be next."

Estelle snorted. "Nah, he's still besotted with... what's her name? Flora. Anyway, good luck getting Cass to admit to being at the beach if she won't even share her romantic entanglements with her family."

"Fair point." At that moment, a group of students entered the library, and I abandoned the notion of talking to Cass for the time being while we dealt with their requests for study aids. With three of us at the desk, dividing the various tasks between us was easier. I didn't see Marla Hutchins or her friends among the students who came to us for help, though I doubted she wanted to risk another close encounter with the Artefacts Division. I was also willing to bet they hadn't been out partying at the beach again the previous night, but I knew someone who had.

When I had a spare moment, I climbed the stairs to the third floor to look for Cass. The odds of her willingly answering my questions were as high as her being thrilled to hear I'd spoken to two of her ex-partners, but it seemed ridiculous to talk to the werewolf pack and not the one person who'd certainly been near the beach at some point last night.

I made my way through the rows of shelves and followed the faint scent of animal dung to the corridor where Cass spent most of her time. The door was locked. No surprise there.

I rapped my knuckles on the wood. "Cass, I need to talk to you. Were you at the beach last night?"

Her muffled reply came through the locked door. "Who wants to know?"

"I do, and I won't tell everyone if you don't want me to."

She scoffed. "Yeah, right. You'll only tell our entire family, plus your familiar, who'll spread word to the entire town."

"So, you *were* out, then?"

She didn't answer.

"Cass, seriously." I dropped my voice. "If you knew anything about the noises the inn's guests heard last night, you'd tell the police, wouldn't you? Especially if they belonged to something dangerous."

No reply.

"I hope that means yes." I racked my brains for a comment that might prompt a response. "Also, I spoke to the shifters. Your ex's brother."

"What's it to you?"

At least she'd responded, if not in a particularly helpful way. "I think the shifters might have seen the creature, but they wouldn't admit it."

Another prolonged pause.

"Cass," I said, exasperated. "I meant it. I'm not planning

on telling anyone if you want my help. Not if you don't want me to."

Silence. A dismissal if I ever heard one... or rather, didn't hear one. I didn't know why I'd bothered trying to get through to her, but I was sure she *did* know something about the mystery monster. That she didn't trust me enough to share it with me was understandable, if annoying.

Okay, time for an alternative strategy.

I turned away from the door and walked back to the stairs, doing a double take when I spotted Sylvester perched on the balcony overlooking the floors below.

"Sylvester." I halted next to him. "Did Cass tell *you* whether she was at the beach last night or not?"

"Now, do you think I'd give away what she told me in confidence?"

I tilted my head to one side. "That means she did go to the beach, right?"

"I was speaking generally. Besides, I have no interest in your dull human affairs."

"Sylvester, you woke everyone up this morning because you wanted us to know the mystery monster appeared again," I pointed out. "That's the opposite of not being interested."

He shuffled his wings. "I won't tell you next time, then."

"That isn't what I meant." I rubbed my forehead. "Why are you here? To talk to Cass?"

"You only get one question."

I blinked. "Are you telling me the Book of Questions is willing to tell me what the creature is? Because that would save me an awful lot of time and annoyance."

Sylvester made a disgruntled hooting noise. "The Book does not exist to save you time and annoyance, you impudent spoon."

I threw up my hands. "Then why even bring it up? Honestly. I might as well keep asking Cass until she finally opens the door to get rid of me."

"Go away!" Cass shouted from behind the shelves.

I jumped. I hadn't known she'd heard us since we hadn't been speaking that loudly... but a sudden rush of dread flooded me. If she'd heard our conversation, then she might have put two and two together about Sylvester's real identity.

I took a wary step back. "Sylvester, does she know what... what you are?"

The owl, meanwhile, had gone ominously quiet, but his head rotated to follow my movements as I backed towards the stairs.

"I'll take that as a no." My heart thudded in my chest. "I don't think she heard everything, though—"

The floor gave way beneath my feet, carrying me downwards into oblivion. Too startled to scream, I tumbled head over heels...

...and found myself in the Forbidden Room.

I lay on my back, breathless, in the centre of the small square room. The blank walls, ceiling, and floor were all the same shade of colourless white, bringing a wave of dizziness at the thought that I didn't really know for sure which way was up or down.

Nor did I know how I'd got in here either. I'd thought the only way to enter the room was through the Book of Questions, and while Sylvester had control over the room, I'd had no idea he had the ability to toss me in here without the need for the book at all. It occurred to me, entirely too late, that Sylvester might have been hiding the true extent of his abilities—a frightening thought.

"Sylvester, that was uncalled for," I told the room at large, sitting up. "It was an accident."

No reply came, though I was sure the owl could hear every single word I uttered inside the room. He owned the Book of Questions, after all, and had complete control over every inch of the room inside the Book's boundaries.

"What do you want me to do?" I asked. "Apologise? I'm sorry, Sylvester. I didn't know Cass could hear."

The owl's voice came out of the blank walls. "Walls have ears. So do books."

"We've never exactly been *that* careful when talking about your secret before, though," I said to him. "You're always dropping hints. If you didn't, I wouldn't have figured it out myself."

Silence responded. I pushed upright, rubbing my sore back.

"Sylvester." The owl was as good at giving the silent treatment as Cass was, if not better. "Why *did* you trap me in here? It's not going to change anything."

"This room can change a lot of things," Sylvester's voice said enigmatically.

"What, you want me to ask a question?" That might convince him to let me out, but only if I picked the right question. Asking the identity of the mystery monster wouldn't help... unless Cass had told *him* what it was. She might have.

I faced the wall. "What kind of creature has been appearing at the beach and scaring people?"

No response came. Instead, the floor opened like the

pages of a book, and I fell out of the Forbidden Room, landing on my back in the Dimensional Studies Section. A book was clutched in my hands, but before I could look at the title, the floor began to move like a treadmill, carrying me along with it. It took me three attempts to get on my feet without falling back onto my rear, and no sooner had I found my balance than I crashed headlong into a bookshelf.

Ears ringing and head spinning, I wobbled to the end of the room and groaned in relief when I found myself near the stairs. Then I looked down at the book in my hands, which definitely hadn't been there before I'd entered the Forbidden Room. Either Sylvester had given it to me, or it'd fallen from a shelf in the Dimensional Studies Section.

Sylvester himself was nowhere to be seen, but I kept both eyes open for him while I made my way down from the second floor, not trusting him not to make me fall through the floor. Once I was on solid ground, I gladly limped to the front desk.

"What happened to you?" asked Estelle. "You've been gone for ages."

"Sylvester." Before he showed up and tossed me back into the Forbidden Room for giving him away, I added, "He intentionally got me lost up on the third floor when I was trying to convince Cass to admit whether she went near the beach last night or not. Somehow I ended up in the Dimensional Studies Section on the way down."

"Huh," said Estelle. "Honestly, that owl is getting weirder and weirder by the day. What's that book?"

"I think I grabbed it at some point when I was on my way down." In fact, it was one of Aunt Candace's bizarre werewolf-cyberpunk adventures. Nothing remotely related to mystery monsters.

So much for the Forbidden Room answering my question. I was inclined to think I'd grabbed the book by accident instead, so I left it on the front desk and tried to ignore the throbbing pain in my back and rear from Sylvester's antics. That owl really needed to get himself a hobby that wasn't winding me up, though I hoped that asking a question had sated his desire to trap me in the Forbidden Room as punishment for potentially revealing his secret.

If Cass *had* heard, was it really a bad thing? The two liked one another, for reasons I couldn't fathom, and it was hardly worse than Aunt Candace learning the owl's true nature. Though if Sylvester hadn't known the nature of the mystery beast, then perhaps they didn't share everything with one another.

Why did he even want me to ask a question in the first place?

"I should probably handle the returns if Sylvester is in one of his moods," Estelle told me. "You can watch the desk instead. Much safer."

"I wouldn't speak too soon. Don't forget those students from yesterday might come back for revenge on me for trapping them in the Magical Artefacts Division."

"Fair point." A grin crept onto her mouth. "That was a genius idea, you know."

"Might have been a bit much, though," I admitted. "Maybe I *am* becoming more like Cass. Or Sylvester."

"They couldn't have actually expected you to cheat for them, could they?" she asked. "Besides, if it was Sylvester who told you that, then he's one to talk. I was starting to think you were having a good influence on *him*. Cass too."

"Me?" I blinked. "I have no control over either of them."

"No, but they were even more unmanageable before you came along."

Huh. I hadn't even considered the possibility of being a good influence, mostly because it was hard imagining them behaving any worse than they already did. "Really?"

"Oh yeah," she said. "Cass would hide in her room for so long that we'd forget what her face looked like, while Sylvester had a habit of speaking in riddles for weeks at a time."

"I didn't know that."

"Yeah, you had a positive impact, Rory," she said. "Don't let anyone make you think otherwise."

I smiled. "Thanks, Estelle. I'll be avoiding the Dimensional Studies Section for the time being, though. It's even more difficult to navigate if you're lying down."

"I can imagine it is," she commented. "I wonder whether this mystery monster is the reason Sylvester is acting out?"

I shrugged, evading the question. "I wish Cass had told me whether she went out last night. It's not as if we haven't already guessed."

"I know." Estelle put on a thoughtful look. "It might be worth asking the guests at the inn whether they saw her. Half the rooms face the beach. You'd think someone would have looked out to see where the noise was coming from."

"I thought the same earlier."

Most of the guests were talking to the police, but there

was one guest who hadn't been anywhere in sight: Robin. She'd certainly been within hearing distance of the beach, and her familiar was curious enough that she was bound to have gone for a look around.

Given my track record that day, I might have been better off leaving the situation alone, but Robin had been the first to put the idea of a shifter's involvement into my head. It might be worth asking and hoping she was more willing to confide in me than Cass or the shifters.

9

At lunchtime, I left the library and briefly stopped off at Zee's bakery to buy a muffin before heading to the seafront. The sun was still out despite the cloudy sky, though I had little doubt that we'd be back to rainstorms before we knew it, and I resolved to enjoy the warmth while I had the chance.

I took Jet with me, and he chattered away in my ear as we walked to the beach. I'd also brought the bag of treats to give him in exchange for obeying my commands, which did seem to be helping despite Aunt Candace distracting him by sending him out in search of gossip. Yet with the weekend looming and the exam on the other side, I could only hope that our preparation had been enough.

While I finished my muffin, I went looking for Robin and Tansy. I'd assumed the guests from the inn would be out on the beach enjoying the weather despite the nocturnal disturbances last night, but I didn't see any signs of Tansy's fluffy red tail anywhere. When I reached the inn, a familiar red flicker caught my eye behind an open window three floors up.

"Jet, can you fly up there and ask Tansy to fetch Robin and bring her outside?"

I assumed she was inside, but this was hardly the weather to be sitting indoors. Unless she'd taken it upon herself to read the entire library book that she'd taken out the previous day, which she might have. From Aunt Adelaide's comments about her influential family, I wondered who else had come with her. They hadn't come to the library, though, and since Robin had almost seen through Sylvester's facade, perhaps it was better that none of her other family members had been there too. Given Sylvester's antics earlier, I was doubly glad she hadn't mentioned anything to his face either.

I raised my head to watch my familiar, trying to forget the prospect of the owl's wrath when I returned to the library. Jet perched on the windowsill, and Tansy poked her little head out of the window, giving a squeak of acknowledgement before disappearing within the room.

Jet flew back down to me. "She's on her way downstairs, partner!"

Raised voices drifted from the open window, including Robin's, but I couldn't make out the words.

"All right," I said. "Jet, can you fly to the police station and let me know if anyone mentions any theories about the mystery monster?"

He took off while I waited outside the inn. A few minutes later, Robin emerged through the front door, wearing an expression of mild annoyance. "Hey, Rory."

"Hey," I said. "I'm guessing you heard the latest?"

"I did." She scanned the beach, Tansy settling on her

shoulder. "Good, the police aren't out. I did wonder if they would be."

"Have you been outside yet?"

"Not for long," she answered. "My mother insisted on me reading the book you loaned me, or as much of it as I can cover in a day or two."

"Your mum's up there?" I indicated the open window.

"Yes, and my brother." Her jaw twitched. "They wouldn't know a holiday if it bounced a beach ball on their heads and pushed them down a waterslide. It's way too hot in that room, so thanks for rescuing me."

"Want to get ice cream?" I indicated the small ice cream parlour just down the street from us. "That ought to cool you down."

"I like the sound of that."

We bought ice creams and ate them while walking along the beach. Robin's mood notably improved.

"This is good," she said through a mouthful of vanilla and lemon. "Want some, Tansy?"

Tansy stuck her tongue into the ice cream and squeaked in delight.

"I think she approves." I scanned the beach, where a handful of tourists lay sunbathing. "Did you hear the noise last night? The screaming? I know you said you sleep with earplugs in."

"I do," she said. "Tansy said she heard, though."

"Did she say whether it sounded like a human screaming, or an animal?"

"Animal," she said decisively. "She woke me up, actually, but I didn't see anyone when I looked out the window."

If she was telling the truth, then the creature must

have appeared elsewhere on the beach. I finished my ice cream, my gaze skimming the sand.

"I talked to the local shifters earlier," I said, deciding to give her as much information as I could spare. "They were adamant the creature had nothing to do with the local pack. I think they were telling the truth, but I'm not sure whether they gave me the full story."

"I get that." She gave the rest of her ice cream cone to Tansy, who crunched it up with enthusiasm. "I'd have talked to them myself if I'd been at home, but I don't know the local pack, and I doubt they'd want me barging in and asking questions."

"Yeah. We found werewolf fur over there earlier." I pointed to the bare tree. "My aunt decided to take it to the police, but the shifters I spoke to claimed it didn't prove anything as shifters shed a lot."

"They do at that," said Robin. "Might be true. So, you had a look around earlier?"

"Yeah, and we found… markings." I indicated the claw marks scraped into the side of the tree. "Might Tansy be able to sniff out if they're recent or not?"

"Sure." She walked behind me onto the sand. "Right, Tansy?"

Tansy licked ice cream off her nose and nodded before bounding ahead of us towards the fallen tree.

"Did any of the other guests mention looking out the window?" I asked Robin. "You'd think someone would have got curious enough to look outside."

"Not necessarily." She watched Tansy's tail flicker up and down the bone-white colour of the fallen tree. "A lot of people would assume a tussle between shifters and go back to sleep."

"There were a bunch of people at the police station earlier, though."

"The story of this mystery monster has taken on a life of its own," she said. "Honestly, I've heard people making all kinds of claims. Some have even said they won't be coming back to Ivory Beach again until they're certain they aren't going to get eaten."

"Seriously?" My heart sank. "But—like you said, the noise fits the description of a shifter. It's not unusual in the magical world, is it?"

A holiday destination with mysterious monsters causing a disturbance on the beaches at night was not a selling point for most people, though, magical or otherwise. With the creature's identity still unknown, it was no wonder rumours and hysteria thrived among the tourists.

"What about that cousin of yours?" Robin asked. "Does she know anything?"

"Cass won't tell anyone whether or not she was out last night," I admitted. "But if she was, I don't see her withholding information that might endanger the public."

"You know her better than I do," said Robin. "But if nobody is coming forward, then someone isn't telling the full story."

Like you? The reaction of the Artefacts Division to her presence proved she had secrets of her own, but I'd assumed they had no link to the mystery beast.

"Someone from the inn?" I ventured. "Do you think any of them might have seen the creature and not mentioned it?"

"No." She shook her head. "They wouldn't have been able to resist telling everyone—what is it, Tansy?"

The squirrel had returned from the tree, and she climbed up Robin's shoulder and squeaked in her ear.

"Tansy said she looked out the window last night after I went back to sleep and she saw someone walking down to the beach," said Robin. "Not a guest from the hotel. She thinks it was a werewolf but in human form. A young man."

"How would she be able to tell?"

"There are a lot of shifters in our town, so she's familiar with how they move," she explained. "She's pretty certain of herself."

Tansy made some more noises, and Robin grinned at whatever she'd said. *A shifter was wandering around... after the creature appeared?* Patch? He'd claimed that he didn't go to the beach at night, but I'd been certain he hadn't told me everything he knew.

"This was after the screaming?" I turned away from the fallen tree and faced the police station. "Looks like the crowd's died down."

Robin eyed the brick building near the pier. "You're going to speak to the police?"

"I think my aunt might be in there," I explained. "She's a writer, so she has a tendency to turn everything into a research opportunity. The police aren't her biggest fans, for that reason."

"She wasn't out last night, was she?"

"Definitely not, judging by her reaction this morning when she heard the news," I said. "She ambushed the police after the incident at the pier as well, so I shouldn't be surprised she's doing the same again."

"Sounds more fun than *my* aunt." She wrinkled her

nose. "I'm glad only my mum and my brother came with me. You don't have any siblings?"

"No, but my two cousins are around my age."

"Thought so. I wish my cousin Rowan could have come with me, but she had to work."

I expected her to make herself scarce when I approached the police station, but Robin and Tansy kept pace with me until I reached the front doors.

Robin sidestepped the automatic doors. "I'll wait outside."

I entered the police station alone, spotting Jet perching on a nearby rooftop. To my alarm, Aunt Candace's voice drifted outwards from one of the doors near the back of the reception area.

"Edwin." I addressed the elf policeman, who stood near the front desk with one of his troll guards. "Aunt Candace isn't in jail... is she?"

"No, she's in the corridor." His jaw twitched. "Despite my request to the contrary, she insisted on following one of my guards in there."

"What questions could she possibly have left to ask?" I shook my head. "Never mind. Did you speak to all the people who came here earlier?"

"Yes, and I'm not going to repeat everything they told me."

Wow, something had put him in a bad mood. Or some*one*, like my aunt. "I've heard several mentions of shifters being sighted at the beach last night around the time of the creature's appearance, so I wondered whether you'd spoken to them yet."

"You mean the owner of that?" He indicated the reception desk, where the piece of grey fur Aunt Candace had picked up lay forlornly on top of a stack of papers. "That is not proof, Aurora."

"I know." I also sensed a losing battle at hand, but I figured I might as well mention the pack while I had the chance. "I'm not saying any of them did it either, but there might be witnesses among the shifters who have yet to come forward."

Edwin narrowed his eyes. "I have shifters on my own team, so I'm well aware that the pack has no knowledge of this mysterious beast."

My mouth parted. While I'd forgotten a few werewolves worked on the police force, the other shifters would not appreciate it if I sent the police to question them when I didn't know for sure if whoever Tansy had seen from the window might be linked to the mystery monster. Besides, she and Robin weren't familiar with the locals, and the guy might have been simply taking a midnight stroll for all we knew. Edwin was right—there was no proof.

"I thought some of the guests from the inn might have looked out the window," I said. "Did any of them report anything other than screaming?"

"It was after two in the morning," he said. "The noise didn't come from directly outside the inn, so no, they did not see the cause. That's all I have, Aurora, and I can't keep sharing the results of my investigation with your family members."

"Who exactly is Aunt Candace talking to?" I asked, wondering who'd chosen to humour her.

"One of my colleagues," he said in an annoyed tone. "Someone willing to put up with her questions, no doubt. Look, Aurora, I don't want to be rude, but this really isn't any of your business. I doubt you're researching for a book yourself."

"No..." But if Cass *had* been outside, nobody had mentioned seeing her. I couldn't betray her trust by admitting that she'd left out bait for the creature in front of Edwin, and she *definitely* wouldn't thank me for telling tales on her to the police. Besides, for all I knew, she hadn't been there last night at all.

"What is it?" Edwin pressed. "Does someone in your family know the beast's identity? If so, Aurora, then I would greatly appreciate it if you told me."

"You know as much as I do." That, at least, was the truth.

"Good," he said. "I'm willing to make certain allowances, based on the library's reputation and usefulness, but I would be glad to know that this unfortunate incident is not connected to your family."

"It isn't."

Wherever the creature had originally come from, my family hadn't brought it to town. I knew that much, but not even the threat of arrest would pry any secrets from Cass.

Besides, nobody had seen her, not even Robin or her familiar. All anyone had heard was a scream—which, if it'd belonged to a person and not Cass, meant there must've been at least one other witness who had yet to come forward.

Edwin nodded. "Good. I will send your aunt back to the library once I'm able to get a word in edgeways. I don't know what George finds so entertaining about her, personally."

Intrigued, I peered through the glass window atop the

door leading to the cells to see who she was talking to. A shifter, judging by his shaved blond head and broad shoulders, but surely not a relation of the pack chief.

"Wait." I dragged my gaze back to the police chief. "She's talking to a shifter? Even though she brought the…" I trailed off when Edwin tossed the scrap of werewolf fur into the bin.

"That isn't evidence, Aurora," he said firmly. "If it was, I'd have to put everything in my office into quarantine for evaluation. Simply having werewolf employees costs a fortune in cleaning bills."

That was a dismissal if I ever heard one. "Thanks anyway."

I rejoined Robin and Tansy outside, and the former gave me a sceptical look. "He's just okay with random people asking questions all day? Because my brother wouldn't stand for that. He's our local police chief."

"Your brother?" I recalled the snooty blond guy she'd been with the first time I'd seen her. "He really does work for the police?"

"Yeah, he's the head of the police in Wildwood Heath," she said. "It's not much fun for the rest of us, let me tell you. That Edwin seems a lot more chilled out."

"You haven't met his troll security guards yet. Anyway, Aunt Candace found someone else to hassle."

A shifter, no less. I'd ask her for the details later, but it was Cass who had me stumped. It was all very well promising to keep her secret, if necessary, but Edwin already seemed to suspect someone in my family was involved, and if he hadn't been referring to Aunt Candace, there was only one other person he might have meant.

"Yeah, true," said Robin. "What are you going to do now, then?"

"I need to go back to the library, but..." I paused. "I wish I knew who the other witness was. The person who screamed. If it wasn't the creature, I mean."

"Yeah." Her brow wrinkled. "If you're up to some midnight sleuthing to see whether the creature shows up again, I can meet you at the beach tonight, but that might not go down well with my mother. Fair warning."

"She's... head of your coven, right?" Given the level of influence she held over Robin, she must be.

"Yeah." A grimace tugged at her mouth. "She's good at her job, but she's as much of a party animal as my brother is. She'll be annoyed with me for taking off instead of sitting in the hotel room taking notes from your library book."

"You should head back, too, then, if you're going to give her the slip tonight."

I didn't care for the idea of doing exactly what Cass did—namely, investigating the creature without the involvement of the authorities—but unless we caught and identified the beast soon, our town would end up with a warning sign above it in every holiday ad in the magical world.

And so would the library.

10

After Robin and I had parted ways, I went back to the library. I opted not to tell Estelle about my half-formed plan to meet Robin and tail Cass to the beach that night in case Sylvester was snooping around in the background, though he remained notably absent despite his antics earlier.

While I was sure I hadn't heard the last of our clash up on the third floor, the rest of the day passed without any major incidents. Even when the students from the day before came to the library, they simply glanced at me and then shuffled away as though scared that I'd order another room to try to eat them. All things considered, it wasn't the worst outcome.

Xavier messaged me while Estelle and I were tidying the library at closing time, asking whether I wanted to go grab dinner at the Black Dog. We hadn't had a date in a few days, so I was more than happy to take the chance to catch up with him. My exam might be on Monday, but I had the rest of the weekend to practise with Jet, so I could afford an evening off.

"You think Cass knows what the creature is?" he asked me, as we sat down at the table in the pub.

"She won't admit to anything either way." I stifled a yawn behind my hand. "Without proof, I'm going in circles. Nobody from the hotel will own up to having seen anything, either, except Tansy the squirrel. She saw a shifter from the window, allegedly, but she's not local so she didn't know who it was."

"You said you met with the pack earlier?"

"I spoke to Patch, the son of the pack chief," I explained. "I wanted his perspective, but he made it clear that if it was a rogue causing these disturbances, the pack would deal with it, and that should have already happened by now."

"No, if it was a rogue, there'd be more clues," he said. "A trail leading to the shifter's hiding place."

"Exactly," I said. "He also admitted he likes surfing at the beach, but I don't see why he'd have been there at two in the morning. This isn't the first time a shifter's been at the scene, though. Tansy—Robin's familiar—sniffed around the pier and said a human was there at the same time as the creature and the scent of a shifter was there too. Perhaps a shifter befriended the creature while they were in their shifted form."

"They might have," Xavier mused. "But that doesn't explain the screaming. Unless it was a newly transformed werewolf. They sometimes find the first shift quite painful, from what I hear."

"Patch said the same, but he was still adamant that the screaming wasn't a shifter."

"I'm surprised you talked to him alone," he commented. "Didn't Estelle go with you?"

"We were understaffed, and someone needed to keep an eye on the two troublemakers at the library," I explained. "I took Jet with me instead to give him experience in following directions. I thought he'd prefer it to being in a classroom."

He nodded in understanding. "I forgot about your exam. How long do you have?"

"Until first thing on Monday morning." My heart gave an uneasy flip at the thought. The days were racing by, and while I'd done my best to cram in every chance to practise into the past week, I'd been hoping the mystery monster case would be far behind us before my exam. "He's made great progress, but he does better out in the field than in a classroom, so I guess I need to figure out how to replicate that indoors."

He nodded. "You can't get everything from a textbook, I suppose."

"Cass would agree." I still hadn't decided whether to go along with Robin's plan to go to the beach later that night and keep an eye out for Cass, but I decided to ask Xavier's advice.

Xavier raised a brow when I told him. "She won't thank you if she catches you."

"I wish she'd just *tell* someone if she knows the truth about the creature—aside from Sylvester." I'd decided against mentioning the incident earlier, not wanting to risk retaliation from the owl. I was pretty sure he hadn't followed us all the way to the pub, but you never really knew. "He'd probably encourage her, if anything."

"Not ideal," he agreed. "I'd offer to follow her myself,

but my boss has already told me in no uncertain terms to stay out of this mystery monster case."

"That figures."

"Can Laney follow her instead?"

"I'm surprised she hasn't already, but she's usually busy with vampire lessons," I answered. "Robin might be up for it, though she mentioned she's sharing a hotel room with her overbearing coven leader mother and her police chief brother, so they might stop her going outside at night."

"That sounds almost as fun as dealing with my boss," he remarked. "What about your Aunt Candace?"

"What... you know, I'm not actually sure when she came home from the police station."

I'd remained at the front desk for most of the day, so I'd have seen her come in. She couldn't still be hassling that shifter, right?

"She was there again?" His brows shot up. "Are you sure she's not locked in a cell?"

"According to Edwin, she decided to question one of the other staff members who was willing to talk to her." I rolled my eyes. "She ought to be back at the library by now."

"You can look for her when we get back," he said. "I'm sure she's fine."

I hope so. Aunt Candace didn't seem inclined to chase down the mystery monster herself, but her new friend at the police station would have grown tired of answering her questions at some point, surely.

We returned to other topics until our date was over, and then Xavier and I walked back to the library hand in hand. As usual, the evening had passed too quickly, and I wished he didn't have to go home to the graveyard. The way he drew out our goodbye kiss suggested he'd had the same thought. My heart fluttered in my chest at his touch—and then I jumped when the door flew open and the alarming sight of Sylvester's huge feathery owl form loomed in the doorway.

"Sylvester!" I pressed my hand to my chest, heart now hammering instead. "What are you doing?"

"Did *you* notice your aunt was missing?"

"Aunt Candace?" Oh no. If even Sylvester had taken note of her absence, then she couldn't have returned to the library after all. "She was at the police station the last time I saw her."

"That was hours ago," said the owl.

"Maybe she went to see a friend." Did she even have friends? "If she's not still at the police station, then… I don't know. Maybe she went back to look for the mystery monster."

"We didn't see anyone at the beach," said Xavier.

"It was dark, though," I pointed out. "She might have been hiding out of sight."

Xavier shook his head. "I can detect people using my Reaper senses, and I didn't sense anyone down on the sand. Or the pier."

"I'll take your word for it on that one." Where *was* she, then? "Maybe I should have sent Jet to follow her around and make sure she didn't run into trouble."

Xavier's brow furrowed. "I can technically track her down myself, but I'm not sure she'd appreciate it."

"Maybe not." Xavier's Reaper abilities let him track someone's location and jump directly there, but if she was inside the nest of a giant monster, that might cause more trouble than it was worth. "Knowing her, she got distracted pursuing a new research opportunity. She's done that sort of thing before. Like attending the vampires' parties to ask the guests questions about the nineteenth century."

I didn't think there was a vampire party tonight—Laney would have mentioned it—but the mere thought set my nerves on edge. The last vampire gathering had ended in death and disaster, and Aunt Candace had certainly been known to take risks with the vampires for the sake of research. But there was no reason to believe the vampires were in any way connected with this mystery monster—or Aunt Candace's current whereabouts.

"I'm sure she's fine," Xavier said. "I can stay and wait for her with you, if you like."

The notion was tempting, but I didn't need to drag him into any more of my family's drama. "It's all right. I'll wait for her. Sylvester's probably overreacting."

If I waited for Cass while I was at it, surely one of them would have to emerge eventually. Though I still needed to confirm whether Robin was still up for going out later that night.

Xavier gave me a final hug. "Let me know how it turns out."

As he departed, I called my familiar out of the library. "Jet?"

"Here, partner." He zipped through an open window and hovered at my side. "Do you want me to find your aunt?"

I hesitated for an instant. "Ah—can you go to the inn and ask Robin whether she's still up for going out to the beach tonight?"

"Yes, partner!" He zipped out of sight, while I ducked into the library and followed Sylvester's owl-eyes into the darkness of the lobby.

"You don't think she's gone after the mystery monster?" I asked him, referring to Aunt Candace. He didn't answer, and I made my way to the front desk, where the copy of the book I'd grabbed on my flight through the Dimensional Studies Section lay where I'd left it. "Was that why you gave me this?"

"I didn't give you anything."

I rolled my eyes. "Right, and I suppose you're equally concerned that Cass might be planning to do the same herself, are you?"

The owl made no reply. I didn't want to push my luck, so I made for the stairs and went in search of Laney. Once I reached her guest room, I knocked on her door a heartbeat before it flew open.

"Whoa." Laney startled back from the door and then caught her balance so fast that her limbs blurred. "Rory, I thought you were with Xavier."

"I was until Sylvester got on my case about Aunt Candace not being here."

"She's out?"

"She's been out since this morning when she went to pester the police about the mystery monster," I explained. "She was talking to a shifter at the station the last time I saw her, but that was hours ago. I think even Sylvester is getting concerned that she's run into trouble, but he won't admit it."

Her eyes rounded. "And... Cass?"

"As far as I know, she's upstairs on the third floor, same as usual." I lowered my voice. "When I went up there to talk to her earlier, she wouldn't admit to going back to the beach last night. I thought I might stay up tonight and see if she leaves when she thinks we're all asleep."

Laney arched a brow. "Do you want me to read her thoughts and save you the bother?"

"Do you think that would go over well?"

Granted, she already seemed to think Laney was reading her thoughts, but breaking into her mind for the purposes of extracting a secret would be crossing a line, especially as Laney was otherwise going to all lengths to learn how to avoid using her abilities on me or my family members.

"Maybe that's why she's avoiding us." A knowing glint entered her eyes. "In fact, that makes perfect sense. She can't hide her thoughts from me, so she's hiding herself instead."

"I don't know. She spends most of her time locked up anyway. It's not that unusual."

Not compared to Aunt Candace, who was usually reclusive and never went out at all, let alone disappeared all day.

"Fair enough," said Laney. "It might be easier than playing guessing games, though."

"You aren't wrong, but I'd like to know where Aunt Candace is, too, and that's more urgent." Jet hadn't returned from checking in with Robin, and I was starting to regret not sending him to find my aunt instead. "Xavier can use his Reaper senses to track someone, but there are downsides. I'm not sure the Grim Reaper would want him using his powers for that purpose either."

A thoughtful look came over her face. "You know, nobody said I can't use *my* powers to track her."

"Can you do that?"

"I can track by scent, at any rate," she said. "If I knew where she was last seen, I could follow the trail."

"The police station," I said. "She might still be in there. In a cell. You know what, let's go and look for her."

Laney led the way downstairs, where Sylvester had vacated the lobby. I saw no signs of his owl eyes in the darkness as she glided out of the library with a vampire's typical grace. I followed at a slower human pace and caught her up outside the door.

"Do you have a lesson tonight?" I asked.

"With Evangeline?" She pulled a face, exposing her fangs. "No. I have to show up to some classes at the night school, but I have an hour to kill beforehand."

An unfortunate choice of phrasing, though not inaccurate given the general topic of her lessons. Given Evangeline's habit of shadowing her would-be apprentice, though, I was already having second thoughts about involving Laney in the hunt for my evasive aunt. I'd been intending to focus on unearthing Cass's secret tonight, but I'd completely overlooked Aunt Candace's ongoing absence from the library.

I quickened my pace across the square while Laney walked ahead of me on swift feet. She wasn't trying to overtake me, but her vampire speed had one setting and it went far beyond the average human's capabilities. While I got far more exercise from running up and down stairs in the library than I had as a bookshop assistant, I couldn't hope to keep up with a vampire.

When we reached the seafront, I veered towards the police station and peered through the automatic doors.

Edwin wasn't in the reception area, though I spotted the giant silhouette of one of his troll guards near the back.

"She's not in there," said Laney. "Her scent is strong out here. She must have left within the last few hours."

"Why didn't she come back to the library, then?" I racked my mind for answers and drew a blank. "If she hit a research jackpot, you'd think she'd have come back to note down what she'd learned."

Then again, she'd already had her notebook with her, and perhaps she'd been faced with an opportunity she thought would disappear if she didn't pursue it right away. The question was, did it relate to the mystery monster, or had she followed some other impulse instead?

"I'll follow her scent." Laney turned her back on the police station and walked along the seafront, pausing in front of the Black Dog pub.

"She wasn't in there," I told her. "Xavier and I would have seen her."

"Yeah. She stood outside but never went in. Wonder why."

"Weird." I watched Laney sniff at the air and then change directions, heading up towards the town square.

After retracing our steps into the square, Laney led the way past the library and into the high street. I kept a wary eye on the top of the hill and the church in which the vampires made their home, but she stopped halfway up the hill in front of a restaurant.

"This is where the trail ends."

"Seriously?" I peered through the restaurant window, and my gaze snagged on a familiar woman with a wild mass of red curls. Aunt Candace sat at a table with a muscular blond man, laughing at something he'd said.

That wasn't the shifter she'd been talking to at the police station, was it?

I took a sharp step back from the window when she looked directly at me—but I didn't have a vampire's ability to move fast nor a Reaper's ability to hide in the shadows. Laney glided out of the way, but I was left standing awkwardly by the door when Aunt Candace walked outside.

My aunt glowered at me. "What are you doing, Rory?"

"Looking for you," I replied. "Sylvester was worried about you."

"Ridiculous," she said. "That owl doesn't give two hoots." She laughed loudly at her own joke.

"Hilarious," I responded. "You were gone all day with no explanation, so how was I to know you were on a date? I'm guessing that's what this is." I gestured at the restaurant.

"Obviously," she said. "But now you've ruined my evening, I suppose I'll ask George to walk me back home."

"That's not necessary." My words fell into empty air as she walked back into the restaurant and the door swung closed behind her.

Laney stepped back into view behind me. "What was that about?"

"She and that shifter policeman, George, must have really hit it off."

"No wonder she spent all day at the police station." She laughed. "That took an unexpected turn."

"No kidding." Another thought hit me. "I wonder whether he knows about the time she dated the pack's beta while pretending to be her sister?"

"She didn't, did she?" Laney stifled a snort. "He doesn't know what he's getting into."

"Tell me about it." I shook my head. "I can't believe she never bothered to call anyone, though."

"Yeah..." Laney's expression stilled, her gaze fixing on a spot behind me. I rotated on my heel, my heart sinking at the sight of a familiar tall, beautiful vampire with glossy dark hair and porcelain skin. Evangeline. How did she always manage to sneak up on me? She'd even surprised Laney, which was no easy feat, but the head vampire was not to be underestimated.

Evangeline studied both of us, a smile curling her lip. "How interesting."

"I take it you're not referring to my aunt's love life?" I figured she'd got the measure of the situation in approximately five seconds, given her ability to delve into the minds of anyone around her.

"It *is* interesting that she'd choose a werewolf, considering she once dated Dominic," she said. "That's not typical of those who take an interest in our kind."

"Nothing about my family is typical," I ground out. "Nice seeing you, but I have to get back to the library."

"Naturally," she said. "Ah, Laney. Were you on your way to your lesson? I think a private tutoring session is in order since you're early."

Seriously? Laney didn't answer, but when Evangeline beckoned, Laney gave me an apologetic look before following the leading vampire uphill.

Wonderful. What was I supposed to do now? I had zero desire for Aunt Candace to kill me off in her current novel for ruining her date, and Laney couldn't come and help me follow Cass if she was spending the night stuck under Evangeline's watchful eye, so I had no choice but to leave her at the restaurant and head back home.

No sooner had I opened the door to the library than Aunt Candace caught up to me. If I didn't know better, I'd wonder whether she had a bit of vampire speed herself.

"Where's your date?" I scanned the square and caught sight of a square-jawed man waving at her from near the high street.

She waved back and then elbowed past me into the library, while I caught the door before it shut in my face. *Does he know about the incident with the pack beta?* I took a wild guess that he didn't, though that was the least of the stack of questions I wanted to ask my aunt.

I closed the door behind me. "Aunt Candace, wait."

She didn't turn around. "Isn't ruining my date enough for you?"

"I didn't ruin anything. Anyway, Sylvester was the one who sent me to find you."

"I most certainly did not," said Sylvester.

I shot him a glare. "You interrupted *my* date by screeching about Aunt Candace being missing."

"I didn't know I was interrupting anything."

I shot him a withering look, my face heating at the reminder of how entwined Xavier and I had been at the time. "Maybe we wanted an owl-free evening. Aunt Candace, you didn't learn anything about the mystery monster, did you?"

She swept past me towards the stairs to her room. "If I did, I certainly wouldn't tell you."

She disappeared upstairs, while I remained baffled in the lobby. "I'll take that as a no."

Sylvester let out a cackle. "I'll have you know that Cass

told me that if you tried to follow her out tonight, I have permission to lock you in the vampire's basement until dawn."

"You—what?" How could she have possibly known? She wasn't a mind reader, and neither was Sylvester. "I never said anything about following her."

"Partner!" Jet came swooping through the open window. "Robin says that she can't come out tonight. Her mother wants her to study the library books before they leave town."

I groaned. "Message received. I'm going to bed."

11

I tried to stay awake to hear if Cass left the library, but I passed out before I heard her footsteps on the stairs. She didn't come downstairs at breakfast time either, though Aunt Candace did. She was in a good mood, humming under her breath, and even her notebook and pen danced in the air at her side.

"Have a good date?" asked Aunt Adelaide, who I'd told about her antics after I'd returned from my unexpected encounter with her at the restaurant. "I'm surprised that you stayed out all day with this George person *and* then went out together in the evening. You must have liked him a lot."

"It's not every day that an interview turns into a date," Aunt Candace agreed, "but George and I had a certain chemistry that made it inevitable."

Estelle and I exchanged glances that signalled how little we wanted to hear about our aunt's chemistry with a shifter. I'd almost have rather found her hiking into the nest of a mysterious monster.

"I wasn't aware that it was an interview," I ventured. "Were you asking the police about their investigation?"

"Did you learn anything useful?" Estelle put in. "About the events at the beach, I mean?"

She rose to her feet. "Not everything is about your mystery monster."

"I thought that was what your interview was about in the first place," I pointed out.

"I never said it was." Aunt Candace grabbed a piece of toast before heading out of the kitchen. "Despite your interference, we had a lovely date, and we're going to see one another again."

"Interference?" I said indignantly "Sylvester jumped at me when I got back from my date with Xavier and convinced me to go looking for you. I didn't even go into the restaurant. If you hadn't stormed out, your date would have carried on uninterrupted."

"You brought that vampire friend of yours with you, don't deny it."

So, she *had* seen Laney, despite her stealthy exit. "She thought she might need to save you from a monster. Besides, you'd have been safer staying put, considering Evangeline showed up not long after."

Aunt Candace sucked in a breath. "You brought *her* with you too?"

"No, she was looking for Laney." More or less true, though I couldn't have said how she'd known we were there. "You know she has a habit of showing up where she isn't expected. Though now that you mention it, the vampires aren't fans of the shifters and vice versa. Does George know?"

Aunt Candace's eyes narrowed. "For your information, George does not care a bit about the nature of my past relationships, and I'll thank you not to bring your vampire friends anywhere near our dates in the future."

She left the kitchen, and I heard her retreating upstairs. *Yeah... she's definitely going to kill me off in her next book.*

"I meant to ask if he knows she has a habit of attending Evangeline's parties, not if he knows about her old boyfriend," I clarified. "I know he's not the first shifter she's dated anyway."

"I gathered," said Estelle. "She's just being difficult. Dominic died months ago, and they weren't together for long, so it shouldn't matter to George that she went out with a vampire for a bit."

"It's the vampires I'm more worried about. Evangeline seemed overly interested in their date." Unless it'd been me who'd snagged her attention—or Laney. "If I were her, I'd watch my back."

"Does she ever?" Aunt Adelaide rose to her feet. "At least this new dalliance of hers ought to keep her from pestering Edwin or hunting for monsters."

"I'm surprised she dropped her interest so quickly," I said. "Were there any more incidents at the beach last night?"

"Not that I'm aware of." Estelle yawned. "Granted, I haven't checked the news yet."

"Neither have I," said Aunt Adelaide. "And if Candace hasn't been sending that familiar of yours scouting for news, Aurora, then it's entirely possible we missed it."

"I'd prefer Jet to stay indoors at night, at least until the exam." Which was in two days' time. I needed to get in some more practise this weekend, but my thoughts were as far from studying as possible. "Have either of you seen Cass today?"

"No, but that's nothing new," said Estelle.

"She shut me down hard when I asked if she had any theories on the mystery monster," I said. "I thought she might try sneaking out last night, but Sylvester said she'd ordered him to throw me into the vampire's basement if I tried to follow her outside."

Aunt Adelaide muttered a curse under her breath. "Did she now?"

"I don't know whether Sylvester was telling the truth," I added. "He also told me to look for Aunt Candace and then denied ever doing so."

"Typical." Aunt Adelaide made for the door. "I'll talk to her later."

Estelle and I went to help her open the library for the day while Sylvester watched us from his perch on a high shelf. Given his bizarre behaviour the previous day, it was a little distracting to have his owl eyes following me all over the place. Finally, I gave up pretending to ignore the owl and approached his perch.

"What are you looking at?" I asked Sylvester. "I take it you don't have an update on the mystery monster today?"

"It was your familiar who brought the news yesterday," he informed me. "Not me."

"You're the one who woke us all up." I dropped the argument. "Where's Cass? Is she in her room, or up on the third floor?"

"Why not look for yourself?"

"Not after what you did to me last time." I regretted

the words the instant they left my mouth. My shoulders tensed when Sylvester hooted at me in warning, but he simply turned his back and took flight up to the balconies.

"What was that about?" asked Estelle.

"Who even knows." I shook my head. "I find it hard to believe he used to be worse than this."

"You'd be surprised."

At that moment, Aunt Adelaide came rushing downstairs. "The corridor's flooded again."

"Again?" Estelle asked. "Did Sylvester drop another mouse down the sink?"

"He's not doing it on purpose, is he?" I asked. "He's been in a weird mood lately. Last night he even threatened to throw me into the vampires' basement if I followed Cass out of the library, so I wouldn't say intentionally wrecking the plumbing is beyond him."

"Why would he do that?" Aunt Adelaide looked disgruntled. "Right, I'll have a word with the owl later. Where is he?"

"He flew up to the balcony." I jumped when the door to the library slammed open, and several students came rushing inside the lobby.

"The monster is back!" yelled a teenage girl with bottle-blond hair. "The beach isn't safe!"

"Back?" Estelle looked between them, as did I. "Did you see it? Any of you?"

"No, but Marla Hutchins did," said the blond girl. "We're all doomed!"

Aunt Adelaide took one look at the panicking students and spoke to Estelle and me in an undertone. "I'll keep an eye on them. You two find out what's going on."

Estelle and I left the library at once, making our swift

way across the square to the seafront without saying a word. A clamour drifted from the beach, where pandemonium reigned. A crowd had gathered in front of the police station, extending down to the beach.

I looked for someone familiar and my attention snagged on George, Aunt Candace's new date. Along with several other police officers, he was attempting to get some level of control over the crowd—without much luck. I kept an eye on the handsome shifter as I made my way through the crowd. "Excuse me, what's going on?"

"You again?" His mouth turned downwards at the corners. "You're Candace's niece, aren't you?"

"Yes." Ah. I hadn't made the best of first impressions. "I'm sorry for interrupting your date last night. I didn't realise where my aunt was, and... anyway, what happened here?"

"Hey!" He turned around and snapped at a couple of teenagers attempting to bypass the security trolls near the pier. "Nobody is to access this area of the beach. No exceptions. Shoo, all of you."

Maybe Aunt Candace might be able to get through to him, but she hadn't left the library after our clash at breakfast. Perhaps she'd come running if I told him her date was at the scene, but he didn't appear to be in nearly as good a mood as she was.

"That was her date?" Estelle whispered to me as we made our way through the crowd towards the inn. "He's a little cranky, to say the least."

"Might have good reason to be." A few people had gathered outside the inn to watch the ruckus, but Robin wasn't with them. I spotted her talking to her familiar near the ice cream shop, so Estelle and I headed in that direction.

"Hey." Robin waved at us. "Sorry I couldn't meet up with you last night. Or maybe not, given whatever's going on here."

"You don't know?"

"I heard a few kids saw a massive creature come out of the water," she said. "It chased them off, and they told all their friends."

"Some of them came into the library," I said. "Has Tansy looked around yet?"

Tansy made a squeaking noise from her shoulder that I guessed meant no.

"There are too many people around," Robin answered. "Annoying, but we'll have to wait until later—unless my mother insists on us leaving town today."

"She wants to leave today?"

"After we return the books to the library." She glanced over her shoulder at the inn, her lips pursing. "I'll try to persuade her otherwise, but the last thing anyone needs is the head of the Wildwood Witches inserting herself into this mystery monster case. I'll be back in a minute."

When she vanished back into the inn, Estelle watched the door close behind her. "The Wildwood Witches... her mother is the coven leader?"

"Yeah, and I can only imagine what would happen if she told everyone that Ivory Beach is a haven for mystery monsters." I shuddered. "We have to figure out what's going on here."

I turned back towards the pier, and my heart sank when I recognised the local wizard from the other day marching towards us with a determined stride.

"You." He halted in front of Estelle and me. "Where's that cousin of yours?"

"You mean Cass?" Oh no. Had she been spotted roaming around the area after all? "She's at the library, where she's been all day."

"Someone left bait out near the pier," he said. "The police found the remains. I'm not letting your family get away with drawing vermin to our beaches."

"We didn't." But had Cass? That wasn't a question I could answer, and I found myself wishing I'd run the risk of Sylvester's retaliation and followed her after all.

"I told the police, you know," he said. "This won't stand."

As he stomped away, I turned to Estelle. "I don't know what that guy's problem is. He claims to be a concerned citizen, but I don't think he was even a witness."

"If Cass *did* leave out bait, though, we might be in trouble," said Estelle. "We should go."

"Exactly my thinking," I murmured. "Jet?"

My familiar came at my command and landed on my hand. "Yes, partner?"

"The mysterious monster appeared again, but Estelle and I have to go back to the library," I explained. "Can you keep an eye out for trouble and come and warn us if anyone mentions our names? Especially Cass's."

As for Robin, her family had to return the books to the library before they left town. Even if Robin was willing to help with our current dilemma, her relatives weren't, so we couldn't count on her help.

While the police began driving the crowd away from the pier, Estelle and I headed back to the library. As we passed by the familiar shop, I halted outside. "I wonder whether Alice heard anything?"

"It's worth asking," Estelle agreed. "Maybe she's even seen Cass."

"I thought they weren't on speaking terms."

"They are… kind of," she replied. "I mean, Cass orders supplies for her pets from the familiar shop, and I think she sometimes goes to Alice for advice on the rare occasion that she needs it."

That was news to me. "Good, that'll make it easier."

We entered the pet shop, where Alice crouched on the floor, tipping food into bowls for the cat familiars.

"Hey, Rory." She glanced up. "Hey, Estelle. What's up? Need more treats for your familiar?"

"No, but… well. There was another incident at the beach, so I wondered whether you'd heard."

"I hadn't," she said. "Has nobody figured out what it is yet?"

"No." I pulled out my phone. "I got a photo of the markings on the pier when they first appeared. Can you identify them?"

I showed her the image of the claw marks on the pier, but she shook her head. "I can name a dozen possible creatures that might have left those marks."

"The students described the creature as huge and covered in fur, but bigger than a shifter."

Speaking of the shifters, one or more of them might have witnessed last night's events too. Would they be any more likely to confide in me than they had been the previous time we'd spoken, though? I had my doubts.

Alice shook her head. "Cass is more of an expert than I am on identifying creatures from their prints."

"Cass," I repeated. "Ah—have you seen her around recently? I know you haven't been to the beach, but she's being a bit elusive, and I think she's hunting the monster by herself."

"Sounds like her." She looked distinctly uncomfortable.

"The problem is that she left out bait for it and some other people found out." Cass wouldn't be thrilled with me for telling her, but if anyone would understand, it was Alice. "They told the police too."

Alice bit her lower lip, then said, "Please don't mention this to her, but you should probably know that Cass came in here the other day looking for supplies to feed a large creature of some kind. I did wonder if that might be why."

My heart sank. "She did?"

"Yeah," she replied. "Usually, she orders her supplies to be delivered directly to her at the library, but this time she seemed to want to avoid anyone else seeing."

Estelle and I exchanged glances, her brows rising.

"What kind of supplies?" I asked. "Is that where she got the raw meat?"

Alice inclined her head. "Yes, but that's the only time I've seen her. I'm sorry I can't be of more help."

"Thanks for telling us anyway."

Estelle and I left the familiar shop and crossed the square to the library.

"We have to talk to Cass," I said. "I know I'm probably not the right person…"

"Neither am I," Estelle said. "Sylvester *might* get through to her, but based on the way he's acting at the moment, it's anyone's guess. Cass, though… she has to come forward and admit to what she's doing before someone gets hurt. It's past the point of us being able to brush this off."

"Exactly," I said. "Let's think of confronting her as like taking an injured magical monster to the vet."

Similarly, the best outcome we could hope for was that we all escaped without too many scratches.

12

Our return to the library brought another unwelcome surprise.

"There you are," said Aunt Adelaide. "I was starting to wonder if you ran into Cass."

I groaned. "Don't tell me she went out again."

"No," she replied. "In fact, I'm not entirely sure she's been back to the library since she went out last night."

My heart dropped. "We just spoke to Alice, who admitted she sold Cass supplies she might have fed to the mystery monster."

Aunt Adelaide groaned. "Please tell me someone's figured out what it is."

"The police wouldn't talk to us," I explained. "Aunt Candace's new boyfriend refused to let us know what was going on."

"Did he now?" She looked over at the living quarters as if contemplating dragging Aunt Candace downstairs to ask her to sweet-talk him into answering our questions.

"Typical. This isn't the first time Cass has vanished overnight, but I doubt *she's* on a date."

"Laney offered to read her mind," I admitted. "But it might be too late for that approach now... although she can track her by scent if necessary."

"We'll save that option for later," Aunt Adelaide said. "This has gone too far. I'll get Candace."

While Aunt Adelaide made for the stairs, I found my gaze drifting towards the students who'd gathered in the Reading Corner at the back of the ground floor. While none of them had been witnesses this time around, maybe they'd picked up a hint or two. Like Cass's whereabouts, for instance. She hadn't been at the beach, that I'd seen.

"I'm going to ask a few questions," I told Estelle. "Back in a minute."

"Can't hurt," Estelle replied. "I'll watch the desk. I guess the flood upstairs will have to wait."

I'd forgotten the latest flooding incident upstairs. If Sylvester had been responsible, it was beyond me to figure out why, but he'd known Cass would be going out the previous night. Did he also know her current whereabouts?

I saw no signs of the owl near the Reading Corner, though several students gave me wary looks, perhaps having heard about the incident in the Magical Artefacts Division.

"Hey, can I ask a question?" I asked the nearest group of students, among whom was the girl who'd thanked me for confiscating Marla's speakers. "Does anyone know what exactly happened last night?"

"Marla's telling stories again," said the girl with the

pixies on her glasses, rolling her eyes. "Difference is, this time people believe her."

"Do you?" I looked at her companions, some of whom shook their heads, while others looked a little uneasy. "What did she do, throw another party on the beach last night?"

"She's not lying." The person who answered was the blond girl from earlier who'd burst into the library proclaiming there were monsters on the beach. "Everyone who was there says the same. They're even telling the police."

"Are they at the police station now?" I asked.

"Dunno. Might be."

Unease slid down my spine. "Thanks anyway."

Leaving the students, I returned to the front desk and heard Aunt Candace's voice drifting from the living quarters. "I will not spy on my almost-boyfriend!"

"Almost?" I raised a brow at Estelle. "Am I the only person who thinks the timing is weird? She met this guy when she was pestering the police for an interview, and he seemed pretty intent on driving anyone else away from the beach earlier."

"I don't know about weird timing, but he must really like her to have put up with answering her questions," Estelle said. "He didn't seem friendly earlier, but that's to be expected, given the level of chaos the police are dealing with at the moment."

"Unless he thought I ruined their date like Aunt Candace does," I added. "Honestly, it's Sylvester's fault for panicking me."

"That owl." She tutted. "He's impossible."

"I thought—he might know where Cass is." I might

have said more, but anything that might hint at his true identity would earn me another trip into the Forbidden Room. I didn't have time for that. "Not that he'd admit it."

"True," she said. "I really hope the police are making headway finding the beast if the students have actual reports to give them."

"I hope their descriptions are better than they were last time," I said. "As for Cass, even the police might not be able to track her down if they want to question her."

Estelle shook her head. "I hope they don't take that guy's claims about her leaving bait out seriously, but you're right. I just wish *we* could track her down. I find it hard to believe she was alone out there too."

"I know at least one of the shifters was out the other night," I said. "Not sure about last night, but if Cass was out at the same time…"

"You want to ask them again?" She guessed. "Go on, I'll watch the desk. My mum will give up on trying to get Aunt Candace out of her room soon enough."

She was probably right, unfortunately. "All right. I'll take Jet with me again."

After leaving the library, I called to my familiar, but he didn't answer me. Maybe he'd got distracted at the beach earlier, so I walked to the seafront to find him.

By this point, the police had managed to gain some control over the crowd. The onlookers had mostly dispersed, and while some remained, I didn't see Robin or Tansy among them.

Near the pier, one of Edwin's troll guards spotted me and gave a cheery wave. "Rory, I'm afraid I can't let you onto the pier. Beach is closed too."

Despite how scary they looked, with their huge bodies

crammed into too-small police uniforms, the troll guards were generally pretty friendly guys. Yet I had no doubt they wouldn't hesitate to snap into action if they were faced with the news that Cass was missing and potentially in pursuit of the mystery monster. I glanced towards the police station and saw Edwin talking to a couple of youngsters, but no sign of a blond shifter policeman. "Erm... where's George?"

The troll scratched his lumpy head with a hand. "Why?"

"My Aunt Candace went on a date with him yesterday." Though it didn't sound like she was willing to push him into helping us. "Never mind."

I'd only make things worse if I mentioned what Cass had been up to, and I needed to talk to the shifters before anyone else. Assuming they were willing to talk to *me*, but if they knew where the creature was hiding, then they might know Cass's location. As for my familiar, I saw no signs of him on the rooftops, only a few seagulls overlooking the beach.

Where is he? The troll was starting to look at me with suspicion, so I left the seafront and followed the same route to the shifters' part of town as I had the last time. Jet might have got distracted or even gone looking for Cass, but I could only handle one disaster at a time. I'd talk to the shifters first and hunt for my familiar after I'd confirmed what they knew.

I quickened my pace until I reached the wide house belonging to the werewolf chief, at which point I came to a halt. If the chief himself answered the door and not his son, I'd have a hard time explaining my presence here without inadvertently coming across as accusing the pack of being involved in the creature's attacks. Who else could I possibly ask, though? Crossing my fingers behind my back with one hand, I knocked on the door.

Patch answered, to my relief. "Rory. Back already?"

"Hey." Nerves swarmed me as all my rehearsed questions fled my mind. "I... this is a weird question, but have you seen my cousin Cass?"

"Cass?" he repeated. "No, why? I doubt she's in our part of town."

I weighed the odds. "Maybe not, but I think she went looking for the mystery monster last night, and nobody has seen her since."

His expression flattened. "And why do you think I'd know where she is?"

The sudden hint of hostility in his voice left me tongue-tied. "I—not you, necessarily, but your brother. I know they were close."

"Not anymore," he said. "I think you should go."

My heart sank. "Look, I'm not trying to accuse anyone, but someone I know sighted a shifter on the seafront two nights ago, the same night they heard that screaming—and I think Cass might have been there too."

"Was she now?" Another masculine voice spoke, and a muscular shifter walked into the room behind Patch. I knew in an instant that they were brothers. Family resemblance aside, the newcomer's recognition of my cousin's name meant he could only be her ex-boyfriend.

"Logan," said Patch. "I didn't know you were listening in."

Logan ignored his brother. "Why are you talking about Cass?"

"I thought she might be here." The lie sounded false to

my own ears. "She's missing. She—I think she went looking for that creature at the beach last night and never came back."

"Why would you think we were involved?" Logan took a threatening step forwards. Unlike his brother, the hostility was instantly readable in his expression. "You think we're hiding her, do you?"

"I don't." This was all going wrong. "Someone I know sighted a shifter at the beach the other night, and I have reason to believe she was there as well. Cass was. The person who told me isn't local, so she doesn't know which shifter she saw, but she wouldn't lie." Or would she? Did I really know Robin at all?

"Who told you that?" Logan demanded.

I took a wary step backwards. "Forget it. This was a mistake. I just didn't know who else to ask. My cousin has been missing for at least twelve hours, and since you knew one another, I came here before asking the police."

"You didn't tell the police?" Logan raised a brow.

"They're a little busy with the aftermath of the last mystery monster sighting." I backed up another step. "Like I said, I'm not here to pick a fight with the pack chief. Forget I was here."

Patch levelled a stare at his brother. "Knock it off. We might as well tell her."

"Tell me what?" I halted on the brink of opening the door. "You know where my cousin is?"

"No, but I can guess," Logan growled. "She's persistent, isn't she?"

"You might say that." Wait. "You know where she might be... so you knew she was looking for the beast?"

"Obviously," Logan said. "It's her thing."

"You knew about the mystery beast from the start," I guessed. "But you didn't want her involved?"

Logan made a disgruntled noise. "She wouldn't quit, not even when I asked Patch to chase her off the other night."

"You did *what?*"

"She was setting out bait for the creature, so I chased her off," Patch said sheepishly. "I'm not proud of myself for scaring her, mind."

So it was *her screaming?*

"If she went back, it clearly didn't put her off," added Logan.

I frowned. "Did you do the same to those drunken students the other night?"

"No, but I'm starting to wish I had," Logan said. "Too many people are poking their noses into this mystery beast nonsense."

"It's not nonsense," I protested. "Tons of people are panicking, the tourists are making plans to leave town and tell the magical world at large, and my cousin is *missing.*"

"She isn't," Patch said. "She—"

The sound of someone clearing their throat at my back silenced him. Dread gripped me, and I rotated on my heel as none other than Evangeline came walking up the gravel path to the door. "Excuse me? May I speak to your chief?"

"He's busy," Logan ground out.

"I'm sure he can make time for me," Evangeline said in pleasant tones. "At least ask him, won't you?"

Logan glared daggers at me as if I was somehow responsible for Evangeline being here instead of utterly confounded at her appearance. She wanted to talk to the werewolf chief? I'd thought they were unfriendly at best, mortal enemies at worst. Unless she reserved that status for the Grim Reaper alone, but it was beyond me to figure out *why* she'd picked this particular moment to visit.

Had she read something from my mind and used it to discern that the shifters were involved with the mystery monster? I didn't dare ask in front of the two shifters, though Patch seemed more bewildered than angry.

"I'll let him know," he told the vampires' leader. "If he's around, that is."

While he departed, Logan kept glaring at me until I lowered my gaze. "Sorry, I'll go."

Nobody stopped me, though Evangeline cast an enigmatic smile in my direction as I left. *What is she playing at?* Since when was she even on speaking terms with the head of the local werewolves? If I didn't know better, I'd say she'd barged in for the purposes of derailing me.

I'd have no chance of getting near the shifters and tracking down my cousin after this, which Evangeline must have known full well since I hadn't been shielding my thoughts when she'd sneaked up on me. Staying here would solve nothing, though, and I could always come back later to ask Patch and Logan for the rest of their story.

I didn't bother to avoid the vampires' church on my way back to the library, hurrying down the high street and then across the square. Once inside the library, I faced Aunt Adelaide. "You aren't going to believe—"

I cut myself off when I saw they had company. Robin stood in the entryway, Tansy perched on her shoulder, but she wasn't alone this time. A stern-looking witch who wore her blond hair in a tight bun stood at her side, an orange-and-white cat prowling at her heels, and on her other side was the blond man from before. Somehow, the hedgehog perched on his shoulder didn't make him look any less intimidating.

"You must be Aurora," said the older woman. "I am Lady Wildwood, leader of the Wildwood Coven, and these are my two children, Robin and Ramsey."

"Ah—Robin and I have met." I looked at Aunt Adelaide in puzzlement, but her expression remained grim and gave nothing away. Estelle was nowhere to be seen. Upstairs dealing with the flood, perhaps.

"We came to return the books we borrowed." Robin shifted from one foot to the other in obvious discomfort. "Thank you for the help."

"Interesting place, this." Her mother indicated the library with a sweeping gesture. "The result of a Manifestation curse, is it?"

How does she know? I supposed being a coven leader gave one access to that kind of information, but I'd thought the library was unique in the magical world.

"Yes, my mother's," Aunt Adelaide responded in a crisp tone.

"And registered, I assume," said the blond man, Ramsey. "You might not know this, but I'm the head of law enforcement in Wildwood Heath, and there are a number of things about this library that I find to be matters of great concern."

Aunt Adelaide's mouth thinned. "Oh, is that so?"

"Yes," he said, his tone serious. "The sheer volume of spells contained within this building is volatile enough to prove dangerous to anyone who ventures within."

"We've passed every safety inspection with full marks," Aunt Adelaide told him. "Feel free to look them up."

"I certainly will," said Lady Wildwood. "As the leader of the Wildwood Coven, I have to set a certain example to my fellow witches, and you hold the same authority within your own town."

"I'm aware of that," said Aunt Adelaide. "I'll congratulate you on your recent promotion, but the library is the creation of my late and dearly departed mother, and is therefore under the jurisdiction of…"

The rest of her sentence flew right over my head, and I lost track as the two began to converse in magic-related jargon I hadn't a hope of comprehending. I met Robin's gaze, and the widening of her eyes and the slightest shake of her head indicated that she hadn't seen this coming either.

"…is that sufficient?" Aunt Adelaide asked when I tuned back in.

"It should be," Robin interjected. "Mother, I'm Head Witch, and I'd say there's absolutely nothing wrong with the library."

"You're Head Witch?" I asked. *That* was Robin's secret? She held authority over the others, even her own family members, but it seemed they didn't have any intention of letting her exercise that authority.

Her mother flushed bright red. "It's the *law* that matters to me, and I have reason to believe there is a Genius Loci present in this building that isn't registered."

"A *what?*" asked Aunt Adelaide.

"I'm sure a woman as knowledgeable as yourself must know the definition," said the woman. "Perhaps it's disguised, but there is certainly such a being inside the library."

Aunt Adelaide's mouth thinned even further, and anger I'd never seen from her before flickered in her eyes. "Get *out*."

The woman opened her mouth to protest, and a rumble of thunder sounded in the background. A sudden gale swept up out of nowhere, catching all three Wildwoods and pushing them towards the open door. I barely had time to blink before the strong breeze had deposited the three of them on the doorstep, the door slamming behind them.

I stared at the closed door. "Did the library just kick them out?"

Aunt Adelaide blew out a breath. "I haven't had to do that for a while."

"You…" I trailed off, my mind reeling with the bizarre turn of events. "What did they accuse you of keeping in the library?"

"A Genius Loci is the sentient embodiment of a place —its spirit, if you will," she replied. "I'd certainly know if the library had another being within its walls."

The image of a giant owl came to mind. *Oh no.* "How would she know?"

"She doesn't," Aunt Adelaide said distractedly. "Right, her coven has a knack with animals, but I don't see how she could possibly think…"

A rustling movement drew my gaze upwards, and I hastily glanced downwards. Not before Aunt Adelaide had spotted the owl.

"Sylvester." The colour drained from her face. "It can't be—"

In a rush, the owl descended upon both of us, shrieking. A solid force slammed into us like a hurricane, driving us back until we stumbled through the library door.

Aunt Adelaide and I found ourselves on the doorstep, alone. Breathless, I turned towards the door, only to find it bolted.

The library had locked its doors against us.

13

Aunt Adelaide and I spent several minutes trying to pry open the closed door, to no avail. My one consolation was that Robin and her family had already left, so they didn't witness our struggles to convince the library to let us back in. Or rather, to convince Sylvester... though I'd never been more aware that the two were one and the same.

My aunt looked as close to defeated as I'd ever seen her when she finally let go of the door. "We'll have to wait for the library to calm down, I think. I'm glad our patrons already left, or else we'd have a lot of explaining to do to those students' parents."

"I'm sorry," I murmured. "I shouldn't have—I mean, I didn't know Robin's family were that likely to threaten the library."

"You couldn't have known," she said. "I assumed they were here on holiday, not to pass judgement on our management skills."

"You won't get into trouble for kicking them out?"

"No, but we might find ourselves unpopular with any other major covens who might want to pay a visit." She heaved a sigh. "And I doubt we'll be greeted with open arms if we decide to pay a visit to Wildwood Heath."

"I don't think Robin was pleased with her family members in the slightest, though," I said. "She's the Head Witch even though she isn't the leader of her coven?"

"Apparently so," said Aunt Adelaide. "It's not a position chosen by an election like a coven leader is. A Head Witch is selected by a process involving a ceremonial sceptre, a magical wand with a will of its own. It's the sceptre that chooses the Head Witch."

"So, this sceptre chose Robin?" I surmised. "Is that why she wanted to look up magical artefacts?"

I should have asked, really, but knowing her real title wouldn't have made a difference to her family's intentions. They'd been set against the library from the start.

"I imagine so," she said. "As for Sylvester..."

"A... Genius Loci?" I tested the words in my mouth. "Is that what he is?"

Aunt Adelaide gave me a weary look. "I wish you'd told me."

I blinked at her, lost for words. "Huh?"

She exhaled. "You knew, didn't you?"

"I... I didn't know what he was called." Excuses skittered around my mind. "He told me not to tell anyone since I only found out he wasn't an owl by complete accident. When I came close to giving his secret away in front of Cass, he even shut me in the Forbidden Room then tossed me into the Dimensional Studies Section as an incentive to keep my mouth shut."

"He did *what?*" she asked. "I always made allowances

for the owl based on my mother's attachment to him, but I'm starting to think that was a mistake. I feel like I should have guessed he was more than a familiar."

"I figured he'd tell you all when he felt like it," I said. "I know that's no excuse, though. I should have told you."

"Rory, I don't blame you a bit," she said. "It's all on him. But I don't know what he did to lock us out. I think he might have drawn on the very magic that my mother put into place when she originally cast the spell that created the library."

My heart dropped. "So we can't get in. Does that mean the others can't get out?"

Estelle was still in the library, and so was Aunt Candace. Not to mention Laney. Everyone except the two of us and Cass, who might be anywhere. I'd really screwed up.

"It seems so," said Aunt Adelaide. "At least until Sylvester calms down enough to forgive us. For now, you might as well tell me what you discovered."

"Not as much as I wanted to." I lowered my gaze, shame burning my cheeks. "I think both Patch and Logan know the identity of the mystery monster, and they also knew Cass was looking for it and tried to put her off. Before they could give me any more information, Evangeline, of all people, showed up to visit the pack leader and pretty much bullied me into leaving."

"Evangeline?" Her eyes widened. "What does *she* want with the pack chief?"

"I have no idea, but her timing is terrible," I said. "She did the same thing last night when she ambushed Laney and me when we were looking for Aunt Candace. If she hadn't, Laney and I might have been able to follow Cass when she left the library."

She tutted. "My sister continues to have odd taste in romantic partners. If she's unable to leave the library by their date tonight, then someone will have to give him an excuse."

I hadn't even thought of that. "Oh no. Evangeline won't be thrilled if Laney doesn't make it to her lesson this evening either."

The last thing we needed was for the head of the vampires to find out we'd lost control of our own library. If Sylvester's secret spread to *her*, then he'd be even less likely to forgive the rest of us than he already was.

What an utter mess.

Aunt Adelaide shook her head. "Cass needs to be our priority. I'm guessing the pack members you spoke to weren't overly concerned with her safety?"

"They weren't acting as if she was in imminent danger," I allowed. "I was going to head back and talk to them again, but Evangeline might still be there. If she finds out the library has locked its doors against us, I don't know what the outcome will be."

"I'll risk it," Aunt Adelaide said firmly. "Rory, it's up to you if you want to come with me. I'll head there now."

"I…" *I'm pretty sure the werewolves blamed me for the head vampire being there in the first place*, I wanted to say, but yet another issue came to mind. "I should mention I can't find Jet either, but if he was in the library, he might be trapped in there as well."

Her expression softened with sympathy. "You should find Xavier and explain. I'm sure he'll be willing to step in and help. We might need his assistance to find Cass—if his boss allows it, of course."

"Not a bad call," I acknowledged. "I'll see if he's around. If not, I'll come and find you."

I walked towards the cemetery, which remained shrouded in darkness even during the day. Such was my level of distraction that I didn't think to feel particularly nervous as I pushed open the metal gate and made my way past the rows of overgrown graves to the house at the back.

Luckily, it was Xavier who answered the door and not his boss. "Rory? Something wrong?"

"You might say that." I gave a humourless laugh. "Too much to put into a text message, anyway. I need somewhere to hang out for a while."

His expression turned serious. "My boss is out, but he's supposed to get back soon, and I don't think you want to be here when he does."

"We can go for a walk, then."

Xavier stepped out of the house, sliding his hand into mine. "Did you and Cass have an argument?"

"Worse—she's missing." I scrambled to figure out how to begin explaining the situation. "The library has locked me out, Cass has been gone since last night, and when the werewolf chief's sons were about to explain where she might have disappeared to, Evangeline decided to show up. Also, my aunt is dating one of them. The werewolves, I mean."

"Wow," he said. "The library has locked you out? How?"

"I... have no idea how to explain, to be honest." Even faced with Xavier's comforting touch, my instincts advised against revealing Sylvester's secrets, but it hardly mattered at this point. "Long story short, Robin's family decided to accuse the library's magic of being against coven regulations. Her mother is the leader of the Wildwood Coven and is kind of a big deal in her community."

He gave a low whistle. "I bet the library didn't like that."

"Not a bit," I said. "We'll get back to that later, but Aunt Adelaide and I are locked out and Estelle and Aunt Candace are locked *in*. And Cass and my familiar are both missing."

"You said Cass disappeared last night?" he asked. "She went looking for the monster again?"

"Yeah, and Sylvester covered for her." I grimaced. "Robin was going to come with me to keep an eye on things at the beach, but her family intervened, and I might have taken Laney with me if Evangeline hadn't hauled her off to a private lesson."

"Did you say Evangeline is with the *werewolves*?"

"I have no idea why she showed up there, except to be a nuisance," I muttered. "She ambushed Laney and me when we found my aunt on a date with a werewolf at a local restaurant yesterday after assuming *she'd* gone missing. Maybe she wants to ensure my aunt isn't sharing vampire secrets with the pack. It's as good a guess as any."

"Your aunt wasn't looking for the mystery monster, then?"

"She seems to have dropped the idea," I explained. "But Cass hasn't. Aunt Adelaide has gone to talk to the shifters to see if they know where she is."

"Which shifters?" he asked. "You mean the chief's son?"

"You've got it," I said. "And his brother. Patch even

admitted to chasing her off the other night. That's what the screaming was."

"Seriously?" Xavier's hand gripped mine. "Are you sure you don't want to look around the beach to see if Cass might be there?"

"The police were herding people away earlier," I said. "I guess we might as well have a look while I wait to hear from my aunt, though."

The two of us veered towards the seafront, where the pier remained cordoned off. The police had successfully dispersed the crowd, but the few people on the beach stood in wary huddles, not sitting on the sand enjoying a nice day as they normally would.

"If the mystery monster is living somewhere out at sea, Cass can't be in its lair," I remarked. "Even she can't breathe underwater. Not without the aid of a spell, anyway, and she's been gone for fifteen hours at least."

"True." Xavier cast his gaze over the expanse of sand. "I can't sense her anywhere nearby. Why didn't you go with your aunt to talk to the pack, anyway?"

"I'm pretty sure they blame me for bringing Evangeline to their doorstep." My throat closed up. "Also, I made a major mistake, and my entire family might pay for it."

"What mistake?" Concern entered his tone. "Rory?"

"I kept a secret from them," I whispered. "But Robin's family found out before I could figure out how to tell my aunt and the others. They're experts on any kind of magic relating to animals and familiars—and they claimed the library was dangerous because there was something called a Genius Loci living inside it."

He blinked. "I have no idea what that is."

"Neither did I, but my aunt told me a Genius Loci is

kind of a spirit that embodies a place," I said. "When my grandma cast the spell that created the library, I think she bound its knowledge into a sentient form without telling anyone else."

"Sentient?" he echoed. "You mean a person?"

"Not a person, but close."

"Who…" His eyes widened. "Sylvester."

"Exactly," I said. "I worked it out by complete accident a few months ago, but he made it clear he didn't want me to reveal his secret to everyone else. I didn't know it wasn't legal, what my grandmother did."

"That's why the Forbidden Room can answer all your questions?" he said. "It contains all the library's knowledge… or Sylvester's."

"Exactly." I heaved a sigh. "It's not reliable all the time, but I knew that Sylvester would never let me keep consulting the Book of Questions if I betrayed his trust. Now I'm starting to think I should have taken the risk."

"It's not your fault," he said. "Sylvester is the one who pushed you into the position you ended up in. Where is he?"

"Gone," I muttered. "The library itself locked its doors against us. Aunt Adelaide seemed to think it'll calm down eventually, but now the two of us are trapped on the outside, and we don't know where Cass is. And Jet has me worried too."

"When did you last see him?"

"I asked him to keep an eye out for trouble around here." I gestured at the buildings on the seafront. "I wanted him to let me know if Robin left the inn, but he didn't warn me her family intended to come to the library."

"Strange," he said. "Robin seemed nice, from what you said."

"She is, but her mother... if most coven leaders are like her, I'm glad my family doesn't belong to one." I looked up at the inn, seeing no sign of so much as a single black feather nearby—but I *did* see a red fluffy tail. "That's Robin's familiar. I'll ask whether he's seen Jet."

I walked closer to the inn until I caught Tansy's eye and waved at her. "Tansy, have you seen my familiar anywhere? He's a black crow called Jet."

Tansy squeaked and gestured urgently with her paws, but I couldn't guess what she was trying to say.

"I'll need your witch to interpret for me."

She shook her head and kept waving her paws, mimicking what looked like beating wings.

My heart dropped in my chest. "Please don't say he went looking for Cass."

Tansy gave me a sad look and then scooted up the side of the building again, disappearing through the window.

I took a step back. "We don't want her family to see us. They'll probably drag out the Reaper rulebook next and tell you all the ways you're breaking the regulations."

"They can try," said Xavier. "I'll direct them to my boss."

I choked on a laugh. "Might be entertaining, but we have quite enough to deal with already."

"You aren't wrong," he remarked. "Where do you think Jet went?"

"I have no idea, but my familiar exam is on Monday," I said. "If I don't find him before then…"

"You will." Xavier squeezed my hand. "Where do you

want to go now? Back to the library, or to talk to the shifters?"

"We'll try the library first," I decided. "Maybe one of the others has managed to get outside, or I can try to convince it to let me in. Not likely, but I can imagine Estelle and Aunt Candace haven't a clue what's going on."

I walked with Xavier, away from the seafront and across the square, until I reached the library's sealed front door. Drawing back, I rapped on the wood with my knuckles. "Let me in."

Naturally, the door didn't budge, not even when I pushed at it with all my strength.

"Sylvester, I know you're mad at me, but Jet and Cass are missing," I murmured. "Aunt Candace, Estelle, and Laney are trapped inside the library, and someone's bound to notice at some point. Like Evangeline, for instance. If you don't want her learning your secrets, too, then I'd suggest you open the doors before she comes looking for Laney later this evening."

That was assuming she hadn't already read my mind. Or Aunt Adelaide's, if she was still at the pack chief's house. Whatever the case, the library remained stubbornly sealed against me.

I hammered on the door again. "I thought it was a condition of your magic that you're supposed to protect my family no matter how badly we screw up. Besides, the others didn't do anything wrong, even Cass. Someone has to find her, and if you won't let the others out, then it has to be me."

The door opened a fraction. I grabbed for the handle, but a book came toppling out a heartbeat before the door closed on me again.

I crouched down to pick up the book, which happened to be the title of Aunt Candace's I'd found in my hands when I'd escaped the Dimensional Studies Division. *What use is this?*

"Which book is that?" asked Xavier.

"Aunt Candace's." I rolled my eyes. "It ended up in my hands when Sylvester chased me downstairs after I nearly exposed his secret in front of Cass, but I have no idea why."

"If he was involved, I wouldn't assume it was an accident."

"Fair point, but this isn't relevant to mystery monsters, I can tell you that much." I flipped open the book to prove my point. "It's one of Aunt Candace's werewolf-cyberpunk adventures."

"This one isn't." He picked up another book that lay at the foot of the door, which I was positive hadn't been there beforehand. "Wands and artefacts…"

"That's the book Robin took out." I lifted the book and flipped it open, nearly dropping it when I found a whole chapter on the subject of Genius Loci. "If I'd looked it up earlier, I'd have known the terminology for what Sylvester is. I have to wonder why he let Robin take the book out at all."

"Maybe he knew," he suggested.

"If he had, he wouldn't have flipped out on us when his secret went public."

Then again, he'd seen Robin's talent for himself. He'd known she suspected he wasn't a real owl. Even he surely hadn't predicted that her family would intervene the way they had, but he might have been prepared for something of this nature.

I closed the book. "If we're lucky, he might calm down when Robin's family leaves town, but we don't know when that will be, and Cass is still missing."

"True," he said. "It's not ideal timing either way, but I'll go with you, wherever you want to go."

Gratitude welled within me. "Thanks, Xavier. Have you ever met the local werewolf pack before?"

"Not in person. How are they?"

"I haven't met the chief. Patch is alright, but Logan seems a bit grouchy. Though, my cousin Cass dumped him, and now it turns out she's barged in on their mystery monster situation, so it might be justified. Fair warning."

His brows rose. "I'll take that under advisement. But I'm still coming with you."

With Xavier at my side, I put both books into my bag and turned away from the library. I'd have to earn Sylvester's forgiveness later—after Cass was safely home.

14

Xavier and I walked to shifter territory along the quicker route, up the high street. I glanced towards the vampires' church as we passed, though I couldn't tell whether Evangeline had returned from her meeting with the chief yet. I hoped she had because if *she* learned Sylvester's secret, then it would add another complication at the worst possible time. It was hard to tell whether anyone was at home during the day, though the fact that Evangeline was out and about during daylight hours was doubly suspicious given the vampires' usual preference for the night.

"She's up to something," I told Xavier. "I don't get what, though. She can't be *that* concerned about my aunt's love life."

"Why'd Sylvester give you one of her books, though?" He eyed my shoulder bag. "Which book was it again?"

"The one whose characters got loose in the library a few months ago." I pulled out the book and showed him the cover. "It appeared in my hands after I asked the

Forbidden Room about the creature that had appeared at the beach."

"The book is about werewolves. Maybe it was supposed to be a clue."

I shoved it back into my bag. "It's typical of Sylvester. I was trying to be considerate in keeping his secret, and all he's done is obstruct me at every turn."

That wasn't strictly true, but I had a hard job feeling charitable towards him after he'd shut me out of my home. Not to mention Aunt Adelaide, who hadn't guessed his secret until Robin's family had exposed it. Trying to push the owl out of my thoughts, I walked with Xavier until we came to the large house that belonged to the head werewolf. I kept both eyes open for any signs of the vampires' leader, but while I didn't see her through the open windows, she might have met with him in a more private setting.

"She's not here," Xavier said in an undertone, correctly guessing what was bugging me. "I can't sense her, anyway. This is where the chief lives."

"Yeah, but I didn't see him last time, only his two sons," I whispered. "They're not going to be thrilled with me for showing up again. I think they thought Evangeline followed me. Which she might have, but I can't imagine why."

I knocked on the front door once, and it opened immediately. Logan appeared in the doorway, looking disgruntled. "Not you again. And you brought the *Reaper* this time?"

"I'm looking for my aunt," I explained. "Is she around?"

"Yes, she's talking to the chief," he said. "I've had enough of people barging in here, you know."

"I didn't bring Evangeline here," I told him. "What did *she* want, do you know?"

"I don't, and I wouldn't tell you if I did." He scowled at me. "Just because Cass has taken off—"

"She hasn't taken off."

"—and from what I heard from your aunt, you have a powerful coven threatening your library as well."

Annoyance flared inside me. "The library will be fine, but if the coven in question learns that you've been hiding the existence of this mystery monster, I can guarantee that they'll come after you next. Besides, my cousin is *missing*, and now my familiar is too. Whatever secret you're keeping can't be worth their safety."

He drew in a breath. "It's the creature's safety I'm more concerned with. I'm sure your cousin and familiar are fine, but we can't have any more people disturbing a vulnerable magical beast—including this coven, whoever they are. The Wildwoods, your aunt said."

"They have a special affinity with animals, which means it wouldn't surprise me if one of them has already figured out what this magical beast is." When his stubborn expression didn't waver, I added, "Can't you at least tell me where the creature is hiding so I have an idea of Cass's whereabouts?"

"I can't tell you. I'd have to show you, and if I did, I can guarantee we'd be followed." He ducked back into the house. "This is ridiculous. I wanted to keep this quiet for a reason."

"Who else knows aside from you and Patch?"

"Nobody else in the pack. Or they didn't, at any rate."

My brows rose. "You kept it a secret from the chief?"

"He's not thrilled with us," said Logan. "He demanded

an explanation, but he might wait until he's got rid of your aunt."

"He'll want you to take him to the creature's hideout, right?" I asked. "If so, then you might as well take me with you as well."

"Absolutely not."

Xavier placed a hand on my shoulder before I could object. "I can track your cousin's location myself. It's risky, but I'm less likely to disturb the creature than a regular person is."

"Not if you land on top of it." Would Cass have got that close, though? Knowing her, it was anyone's guess.

Logan's eyes narrowed. "You're going to do *what?*"

"Xavier's Reaper senses allow him to track someone's location," I explained. "He can also keep himself hidden from sight, so he won't cause a disturbance."

A door at the back of the conservatory opened, and Patch walked in. "He wants to talk to you next—Rory's here too?"

"She thinks the Reaper will be able to find her cousin without disturbing the creature's nest," Logan interjected. "I find that hard to believe."

"The Reaper?" Patch's gaze slid to Xavier with a mixture of surprise and wariness, which was pretty standard whenever someone set eyes on him for the first time. "Might work. The creature doesn't mind shifters, so if you're really worried about your cousin, I can go with you."

"No," Logan insisted. "I thought we were going to keep it quiet."

"Too late for that," Patch told him. "Dad knows, and he

thinks word has spread among the others as well. The vampires' leader hinted that that was the case."

"Evangeline?" I frowned. "I know it's none of my business what Evangeline said to your chief, but I don't understand why she's taken an interest in this. What does she have to gain?"

"You tell me," said Logan. "You're the one who's on familiar terms with the vampires' leader."

"I definitely wouldn't say that." So much for avoiding bringing up the subject of my involvement with the vampires with the pack. "This isn't the first time she's shown up somewhere weird in the past day. She ambushed me yesterday outside a restaurant where my aunt went on a date with George. Does *he* know the identity of the monster?"

"George?" Patch's gaze slid over to his brother. "He's been poking around, but I didn't think he'd figured it out yet. Only Cass did, and we hoped she'd let it go."

I turned to Logan too. "I thought you knew Cass. You didn't really think chasing her away would put her off, did you?"

"No," Logan said grudgingly. "I guess not. Wait, you said George was with your aunt? The same one who's talking to the chief?"

"No, my other aunt," I clarified. "She took an interest in the mystery monster, too, so I kind of wondered whether he'd kept her talking all day to keep her from getting too curious. If he didn't know, then I guess not."

"He didn't," Patch said. "Look, if you're going to hunt for Cass, then one of us should go with you."

"I'm not going anywhere," Logan said. "Patch, if you go, then you'd better be careful."

"Always am," Patch responded. "I'll let you know everything when we get back."

Xavier, Patch, and I made a strange group, walking through shifter territory towards the seafront. Patch kept firing questions at me, most of which I answered, though I refrained from mentioning Sylvester, or the reason the library had closed its doors on us. Instead, I placed the blame on Robin's family, which wasn't that inaccurate.

"The Wildwood Witches... I've heard of them," Patch commented. "Bad luck that they took an interest in the library, though."

"Yeah. Like I said, they have experience with magical creatures. I'd be surprised if Robin hadn't figured out what the creature is too."

The three of us slowed our pace when we reached the seafront. While only a handful of people were around, Patch's expression remained wary. "I don't like doing this in daylight."

"The creature isn't hiding close to human habitation, is it?"

"No, but we might be followed." After a final scan of the beach, he led us past the pier and down onto the rockier part of the beach where few people ventured since there was little sand to sit on and the sea washed over the rocks when the tide was in.

I could understand why. The slippery rocks also made our walk slow going, and I had to grip Xavier's arm a couple of times to keep from falling. He never slipped or fell—yet another perk of being a Reaper—while Patch had a werewolf's coordination and was used to moving on all fours in all conditions. Patch halted when we came to a sheer drop, waiting for us to catch up.

"You'll need to use magic to get to the nest," he said. "Your cousin must have done because nobody can climb down without breaking bones or worse. I assume the Reaper can, though."

"No doubt." Xavier peered over the edge. "Rory..."

My mouth went dry at the sight of the sheer rocks jutting out of the water, but I took out my Biblio-Witch Inventory. "My familiar might be down there as well. I need to find him."

I picked out the most likely word—*fly*—and angled myself towards the rocks below.

"Rory." Xavier seized my arm. "Are you sure?"

"Yeah." I'd taken bigger risks in my time in the magical world, and Cass and Jet's safety might depend on my bravery. "I'll be fine."

I tapped the word on my page, and my feet lifted into the air, the spell propelling me forwards. The view of the rocks below became more distinct, and I spotted Cass sitting beside a makeshift nest formed of branches and seaweed and general flotsam.

After flying downwards, I landed gently at her side. Xavier, who'd jumped straight into the water without so much as a splash, came wading onto the rocks a moment later.

Cass whirled on me and pressed a finger to her lips. "What are you doing here?"

"Looking for you," I whispered.

She swore. "Who told you? Logan, right? He's more like a snake shifter than a wolf."

"Patch did, actually, but everything went to hell while you were gone, Cass."

"You—oh, now you've done it." She tensed, her hand

on her wand, and movement stirred in the pile of branches.

My heart jumped into my throat when a *dragon* poked its head out of the nest. The long reptilian head couldn't belong to anything else. Little green scales covered its lithe body, and its claws were hardly longer than my hand.

I sucked in a breath. "It's a baby."

"Yes, and its parents are off hunting," Cass murmured. "You'd better hope they don't come back while you're here."

"And you?"

"I brought bait." She indicated a bag on the rocks nearby. "Besides, I've earned the infant's trust, so its parents will leave me alone."

"Why pick this place as a nest?" I asked, curious despite the worry thrumming under my skin. "Bit close to the water, isn't it?"

"Not too many places are safe for wild dragons," she said. "They typically pick spots close to magical communities, and ours happens to be on the coast. Besides, it was perfectly safe until you decided to disturb the peace."

"You came back here even after the shifters chased you off the other night," I pointed out. "Besides, you can't have expected nobody to worry when you didn't come back to the library."

"I can't leave it alone," she said. "Its parents haven't come back to the nest in over a day. I found it panicking the night before last and promised to help."

"Cass." I understood why she'd stayed, but how could I convince her that she couldn't do anything but worsen the situation by hiding beside the creature's nest? "The library is in trouble too. We need you."

"Not as much as he does." She indicated the infant dragon. "What happened this time?"

"Among other things, Robin's family told us that our library is in breach of magical law, so its magic locked us out. Aunt Adelaide and I are stuck outside of the library and everyone else is trapped on the inside."

"Who the hell is Robin? You know what, I don't care. I'm all maxed out on emergencies."

I had to admit I saw her point, but if she didn't leave the dragon's nest, then we'd run the risk of discovery.

"Robin is a Head Witch, Cass," I told her. "Her mother runs the Wildwood Coven, whose members have an affinity for animals, among other things. I can guarantee they'll figure out where you are, if they haven't already."

"Since when did this have anything to do with them?"

"Their coven is influential enough that they could get us into serious trouble," I went on. "The library itself turned on us, and even your mum admitted that she has no idea how to make the doors let us back in. That's never happened before, has it?"

"No, it hasn't, but knowing your habit of getting us into trouble, I'm not surprised."

That stung. "You're the one sitting in a dragon's nest. All *I* did was try to find you."

"Maybe you should mind your own business."

Typical Cass. When she knew she was in the wrong, she got defensive, but that knowledge didn't quell the spike of anger inside me. "I can't imagine why your ex was willing to tell tales on you."

Her face flushed bright red. "You have some nerve."

I pushed down another sharp remark. "Cass, my familiar is missing too. I didn't just come here for you."

"Jet?" She scowled. "I have no idea where he is. He doesn't know about the nest—which is a miracle, I might add, given that Aunt Candace had him spying for her."

"That wasn't my idea," I protested. "Also, on top of the rest of the madness, Evangeline is primed to take advantage of us being shut out of the library, and your mum is currently talking to the werewolves' chief. I've no doubt he'll be here as soon as he can convince one of his sons to bring him."

"I *knew* you'd bring everyone else on my tail," Cass said. "This is precisely why I didn't want to tell you."

"I didn't bring anyone except Xavier." What would it take to make her see sense? "Look, if I hadn't got involved, Patch and Logan would have come back anyway. They didn't want you here any more than you want me following you."

Xavier tensed. "There's someone else here."

"See what I mean?" Cass burst out. "I knew you couldn't be stealthy if your life depended on it."

I craned my neck to look at the jagged rocks above us. "I don't see anyone."

Water splashed us. I spun around when George the werewolf pulled himself up onto a rock near the dragon's nest, shaking himself like a wet dog.

"I thought you'd be here, Aurora—and you, Cassandra," said George. "Now give that dragon hatchling to me."

15

Of all the people I might have expected to follow us, George was so low on the list he hadn't even registered as a possibility. Now, though, I became abruptly conscious of how much bigger the werewolf was than the rest of us, even in his human form. He must have swum here from the beach, and his gaze showed pure greed when he looked down at the baby dragon.

In the end, all I could think to say was, "I'm surprised Edwin sent you alone."

The shifter shook more water onto the rocks. "This isn't police business. I'm glad Logan and Patch kept it quiet. Edwin means well, but he doesn't understand."

"Understand what?" I glanced at Cass, who'd moved into a defensive stance. "What do you want with the dragon?"

"To sell it, of course. Do you have any idea how much money that creature is worth?"

"Don't you make enough working for the police?"

Xavier asked. "Why would you want to jeopardise your career?"

"It's not illegal to bring in wild magical animals, Reaper." He showed no surprise at seeing Xavier here. "The creature won't be harmed."

That, I wouldn't bet on. It couldn't be more obvious that this guy wasn't looking out for the baby dragon's safety.

"That sounds like selling magical creatures to me, which *is* illegal," Cass said. "I'm not moving."

"I thought not," he said in calm tones. "Even the chief's sons couldn't keep you away, could they?"

"Did you try to follow them?" I guessed. "You did, didn't you?"

"Yes, but they shook me off. That's when I realised I needed to try a different approach."

"That's why you chatted up my aunt?" Incensed, I took a step closer to him. "Did you think she might know how to get near the creature? I assumed you were trying to divert her attention, but that's even worse."

"Almost right," he said. "I asked her for a second date anyway, so it worked out in the end."

"You're despicable," I said. "Does Edwin know you're skulking around here? Or did you sneak off when you're meant to be working?"

"I'm meant to be patrolling the beach." He gave a shrug. "Besides, I imagine he has enough on his mind, with the public's complaints about this monster. Such a fuss over a small creature."

"I'll give *you* a reason to complain." Cass glowered at him. "You aren't taking the dragon."

Another shrug. "I thought I might be able to reason

with you, but it can't be helped." He pulled out what appeared to be some kind of dart gun. *He can't use magic, so he must have taken that from the police station.* If he'd had a wand, he'd have been able to step in much sooner.

"I'd prefer not to shoot you as well, but I'll do it if necessary," he told Cass. "Don't worry, it's laced with a simple sleeping potion, and it won't have any permanent effects."

"Don't you even think about it," Cass warned.

He fired the gun, but Cass's wand flickered, and a flash of light enveloped the small arrow before it could make contact with the baby dragon. The small creature shrieked, wings flapping, but it was Cass who dropped like a stone, a second arrow protruding from her arm.

George moved on the spot, revealing a second dart gun in his other hand. My heart dropped. Cass lay unconscious on the rocks, leaving just Xavier and me between the werewolf and the dragon. The beast shrieked, flailing around its nest, while George gave me a glance as if assessing whether he needed to use a dart on me too.

Think, Rory. "What did you do to its parents? Did you drive them away?"

"I hadn't a hope of capturing two full-grown adult dragons, so yes," he said. "No human can, but a child is manageable with the right tools. Now, get out of my way."

"You can try shooting me," Xavier challenged him. "In fact, you're welcome to. But you won't get near Rory."

Xavier couldn't be affected by the potion, but I certainly could, and George held up his two dart guns. One he pointed at me, one at the dragon.

I grabbed for my Biblio-Witch Inventory, but the dragon fell unconscious in an instant. Xavier moved in a blur, the second dart hitting him in the shoulder. He appeared unaffected, but darkness folded around his hands and formed a blanket of shadow between George and me.

Seizing my chance, I flipped open my Biblio-Witch Inventory. I might have hit any word, but the one my finger landed on was *find*.

Xavier blocked another shot from the dart gun. Growling came from the dragon's nest, and when I glanced over, the dragon shook its head groggily. The dart hadn't entirely worked, but given the snarls coming from its throat, it was furious. So now we had an angry dragon to contend with as well as the werewolf, and even Xavier did not have "taming dragons" in his skill set. As for me, I didn't know the first thing about how to fend off a dragon hatchling *and* an armed werewolf at the same time.

The sound of beating wings came from above our heads. My heart lifted when Jet flew into view... along with Sylvester.

I waved my arms. "Down here!"

The giant tawny owl landed on George's head, causing him to drop both dart guns in surprise. Jet zipped down and pushed both guns into the sea with a caw of delight.

George roared, shaking Sylvester off. Fur sprouted from his skin, his jaw lengthened, and within seconds he'd turned into a massive werewolf. Grey fur covered his body, and his yellow eyes brimmed with fury.

Oh boy.

Now we had a situation on our hands. The werewolf reared up on his hind legs, swiping a claw at the two birds. Both Sylvester and Jet flew out of range to avoid being hit, and he advanced towards the dragon's nest—which was suddenly empty.

The dragon had climbed out of its nest, and when I scanned the water, I saw its little claws splashing. Evidently, it could swim—in fact, I was almost certain it was to blame for the initial claw marks on the pier—but it still must have been dazed by the effects of the dart, and if it sank under, none of us was in a position to come to its rescue.

The werewolf roared in anger, turning away from Xavier and me. He leapt into the water with a splash that drenched all of us—and that was when the dragon beat its little wings and took flight.

I stared at the dragon's small wings beating as it gained height. *It tricked him into going into the water.*

The werewolf roared, but his swiping paws hadn't a hope of catching the baby dragon. It flew straight at Cass and let out a sad-sounding noise at the sight of her lying unconscious on the rocks.

"I know." I faced the dragon but didn't quite dare step closer. "She's unconscious, but we'll help you. If you'll let us."

A flicker of red in the corner of my eye made me raise my head. A red fluffy tail became visible on the rocks as Tansy the squirrel climbed down towards the dragon, making urgent squeaking noises.

"Jet!" I called my familiar down from the sky. "What's she saying?"

The little crow flew and perched on my arm. "She says her family is coming... and so are lots of other people."

Oh no. "Can you tell them to stay back? The dragon's

parents are missing—I think George scared them off—and we don't want to startle him."

"Yes, partner!" He took flight again.

Sylvester had already disappeared, but the dragon was bigger than both of them despite being a juvenile, and I doubted they'd be able to herd it to safety even if the owl had been willing to. The werewolf was fighting a losing battle against the ocean waves, but it was only a matter of time before he reached the rocks again. I turned to Xavier. "We have to stop everyone from crowding the place."

Xavier picked up Cass and slung her body over his shoulder. "I'll get her out of here. Can you use magic to fly up to the beach?"

"Yeah, I can, but I don't like leaving the dragon alone."

Tansy squeaked at me, gesturing with a paw. Wait, she could communicate with the dragon. For all I knew, they'd already met, and I had no choice but to trust her to keep the creature safe from George.

In the meantime, I used the same *fly* spell to ascend the cliffs to the beach, landing on the flattened rocks. Xavier joined me a moment later, Cass draped over his shoulder.

Robin approached us, her eyes widening at the sight of my unconscious cousin. "What is going on?"

"Tansy is with the dragon," I said. "That's our mystery monster, which I assume you already figured out."

A roar sounded. *George.*

Robin took a step back. "That wasn't a dragon."

"No, it's a werewolf who wants to capture the dragon and scared off its parents," I said quickly. "He also shot my cousin with a dart laced with a sleeping spell. The dragon tricked him into jumping in the sea, but—"

A squeak interrupted me as Tansy came running into view.

Robin swore. "She said he got out of the water, and he has the dragon... but how's he going to get up here?"

"Werewolves are good climbers," said Xavier. "But we'll have him surrounded. He must know he has nowhere to run."

Another roar sounded, this one from behind us, followed by a second. Two huge werewolves came barrelling along the sand. I was willing to bet Logan and Patch had heard George roar and had instantly figured out who was responsible.

While they descended the rocky slope towards the nest, a booming voice rang out from the seafront. "Enough!"

Another werewolf—in human form but recognisable as a shifter—walked into view. Huge and muscled, he had the same fair hair as his sons, but his was shot through with grey, and ropy scars stood out on his face and arms. Next to him stood Aunt Adelaide.

This must be the pack chief, and his voice was as loud as a roar even in his human form. "Get up here, now. All of you."

His two sons came scrambling back up the rocks, followed by George's sopping wet furred form. Nobody dared to disobey the chief, not even George—but where was the baby dragon?

"You're a disgrace," Chief Tarquin growled at George. "How dare you go behind my back? Was it worth risking your career and the pack's safety?"

More growling ensued from his sons, unintelligible to me, but George doubtless understood every word. I glanced over at Robin, who'd somehow coaxed the dragon to land next to her. She knelt down and whispered soothing words in his ear, though I was surprised he could hear given the racket the others were making. Maybe she was telling him a story. It wouldn't surprise me at this point.

My familiar flew to land on my arm, chirping happily.

"You have no idea how glad I am to see you," I told Jet. "I thought you'd been captured too."

"Me too, partner!" he said. "I knew the owl would be able to help you."

I looked for Sylvester, but he'd already taken off without allowing me any questions. Probably for the best, considering there were so many people around, but I hoped he'd reconsider sealing the library against us.

A sense of unreality washed over me. The werewolves exchanged growls, while the dragon had curled up sleepily next to Robin, perhaps still groggy from the potion. Trusting that the werewolves would have no need for my help, I made my way over to her. "Hey."

"I'm sorry," said Robin in a low voice. "For my mother's meddling. And my brother's too."

"They aren't here?"

"Not for long, considering the noise we've been making." Her mouth quirked. "Though that's not necessarily a bad thing."

"Why?" I frowned. "Do we really need more people involved? Especially..."

"Especially a couple of meddlers?" She arched a brow. "Actually, they might be the very people who can help track down the dragon's parents. It ought to distract them from the library, though I already made it clear that it isn't within our job description to exert our authority over another coven's property. The most my mother can do is tell the local witch council that it exists, which they no doubt already know."

"Yes, they do." Aunt Adelaide approached us, her gaze dropping to the dragon before returning to Robin. "I'd be willing to discuss the matter with your mother once the creature is taken care of. What happened to Cass?"

I indicated her unconscious body, which Xavier still carried over his shoulder. "George tried to capture the dragon, and he knocked Cass unconscious with some kind of potion. We can't take her back to the library, though."

"Wasn't Sylvester here? I saw him."

"Yes…" I trailed off, not wanting anyone else to overhear the details of our dilemma with the library. Despite the secrets that had come to light recently, we didn't need the entire town to know our business. "All right, we'll take her back."

"Sure." Xavier carried Cass over to join us. "We can see whether your cousin and aunt are around too."

"Good point." The edge of the beach was growing rather crowded, and when Cass woke up, she might find herself in a dilemma if word had spread about her own meetings with the dragon. "Aunt Candace will be furious she missed all the action."

Xavier carried Cass over his shoulder while Aunt Adelaide led the way back to the library. There were few people in the square, luckily, so we reached the doorstep without being accosted.

I pushed against the door first, but it didn't budge an inch. So much for that idea.

"Listen." I addressed the library. "Cass is unconscious and needs help. Keeping us safe is part of your job, isn't it?"

The door remained sealed. I sighed and turned to Xavier. "Maybe if you leave her on the doorstep, it'll let her in. I guess Sylvester isn't ready to forgive me yet."

The door opened without warning, and Aunt Candace appeared in the entryway, her notebook bobbing at her side. "Who locked the doors? I have a date tonight, and I don't appreciate being locked in."

Oh boy. *Who wants to tell her?* From Aunt Adelaide's expression, she was resigned to giving her the bad news, but I had eyes only for the library. I stepped in, tensed in anticipation of a sudden gale pushing me out again—but none came. Instead, Estelle walked into view, her brow furrowing in confusion. "What's going on?"

I glanced at Aunt Adelaide. "It's a long story, but we've got time."

16

"The exam is over," said the examiner, a balding wizard dressed in a long black robe. "You can leave."

"Thank you."

I hope I passed. I left the classroom with Jet, whose wings beat with his usual excitement as we made our way out into the library.

Aunt Adelaide waited for me near the Reading Corner. "How'd it go?"

"You know, it didn't go too badly at all." I reached for the bag of treats I'd left outside the classroom and gave one to Jet, who snapped it up with an enthusiastic chirp. "Jet remembered nearly all the commands, didn't you?"

"Yes, partner!" he squeaked.

"Excellent." Aunt Adelaide smiled at me. "Go and tell Estelle, won't you?"

Jet flew ahead of me towards the front desk, where Estelle sat sorting books into piles. Spark the pixie zipped around the shelves, helping her with various tasks, while Sylvester was nowhere to be seen. Nothing new there.

"Rory," said Estelle. "How'd it go?"

"Good, I think." I waved at the pixie. "Jet did really well."

"I'm glad," said Estelle. "It probably helped that he didn't spend last night spying for Aunt Candace."

"True." I hadn't seen much of Aunt Candace since we'd been forced to break the news of George's arrest, but her absence had given Jet one fewer distraction. Now the exam was over, he had the freedom to gather gossip to his heart's content. "If you ask me, he should get extra points for whatever he did to convince Sylvester to come back and help us."

That was a mystery only the owl knew the answer to… to add to the many others on the list. None of us had heard a word from him on the topic of the Forbidden Room since his return to the library. He wasn't exactly avoiding us, but he never seemed to stay in one place long enough for anyone to ask him a question, and nobody was willing to disturb the fragile peace.

"Yeah, I noticed that the flood upstairs mysteriously disappeared as well," added Estelle.

"Funny that." I shook my head. "I'm going to go with the theory that Sylvester was so concerned for the dragon's well-being that he decided to keep us from finding its location. Unless Cass asked him not to tell us, which is entirely possible."

"She has him wrapped around her little finger," Estelle agreed. "More than even he knows, I think. Did I ever mention they scored top marks in *their* familiar exam without any bribery being involved?"

"Or any exotic animals, I take it?" I rolled my eyes. "I know your mum read her the riot act, but I bet she won't stay put for long. She'll want to reunite the dragon with its parents."

"Oh, Robin's family already found them," said Estelle. "She and Tansy dropped by while you were in the exam room."

"Typical," I said. "Ah—her family weren't with her, were they?"

"No," she replied. "From what I gathered, they have their hands full, what with reuniting the young dragon with its parents then moving all of them to a safer place away from human habitation."

"Cass won't be happy to be left out."

"I think she's already been sending Sylvester to pass on messages to the dragon on her behalf."

"I'm sure she knew what he is." I dropped my voice out of habit, but when I'd told her the news, Estelle had agreed that the owl had been leaving a trail of clues for all of us to see through. If we'd been paying close attention, of course.

In any case, I was glad the Wildwoods hadn't come back to kick up more of a fuss, though Aunt Adelaide had had an extended meeting with Mrs Wildwood and her children at the inn the previous day. I hoped that'd be the end of their meddling considering the dragon ought to keep them distracted for the time being.

I moved in to help Estelle sort through the returns and came across the book Robin had recently returned to the library. "I can take this back to the second floor."

"Are you sure?" she asked.

"Yeah, it's no bother." Not now that I knew what to expect, anyway. I fetched the key and made for the stairs.

I'd wondered whether I might find Sylvester upstairs, but on the second floor, I instead found a familiar group of students hanging around outside the padlocked door.

"And in there, there are *spikes* on the floor and walls," Marla Hutchins was saying to an enthralled audience. "You have to move fast to avoid them, so your spell work had better be up to scratch."

I cleared my throat. "Excuse me?"

Marla whirled around in surprise. Then she raised her chin. "I wanted to show the others the room with the creepy spikes so we can practise spells."

"Right..." I looked in bemusement at the locked door. "I can show them myself since I have the key."

The students eagerly crowded around me as I unlocked the door to return the book to its rightful place. I couldn't fathom why they'd suddenly taken an interest, though deadly spikes were a step up from being chased off by mysterious monsters on the beach.

Before I opened the door, I faced Marla. "Were you telling the truth when you described the beast that chased you off? You said it had fur..."

"Oh." She blinked. "No, I remember now. It was covered with seaweed. Kinda looked like fur, though."

That would explain it. I wasn't complaining about her no longer blasting loud music on the lower floor, so I fully opened the door and stepped inside.

When I put the book back where it belonged, no spikes sprang up out of the walls or floor. My own secrets were old news to the library, it seemed, but that wasn't enough to deter the students. When I left them, they were daring one another to cross the room and hope they didn't get impaled.

At least they'd found a way to entertain themselves that didn't involve throwing parties or being chased by monsters, so I went back to the stairs. I came to an abrupt halt when I spotted Sylvester's owl eyes peering down at me from the third floor.

"Go on," he said. "Don't just stand there staring gormlessly at me."

"You aren't going to throw me anywhere unexpected?"

When he said nothing, I kept a wary eye on him as I climbed the stairs up to the third floor. While Cass was presumably in her usual hideout, Sylvester and I were otherwise alone.

"I'm sorry," I said to the owl, figuring he wanted an apology directly from me. "For giving your secret away."

The owl scoffed. "You think too much of yourself. That Wildwood family has the most annoying magical gift I've ever seen."

"Well… all right," I said. "I assumed you blamed me, given that I was the first to find out."

He huffed. "You're a meddler like they are."

"Sylvester…" I paused. "My grandmother knew, didn't she? She must have."

She was the one who'd cast the spell in the first place, but had Sylvester even existed before then? It was hard to imagine the library without him, but he was too long-lived to have ever been a regular owl.

"You already know the answer to that, Aurora," he said. "There would be no library without me."

"Because you're a… a Genius Loci."

"Correct." He spread his wings wide. "If the Wildwoods want to put me on a list, then they're welcome to try catching me."

The sound of a door opening came from farther back, and I wasn't entirely surprised to see Cass emerge from the corridor where she'd been hiding out.

"Hey," I said to her. "Erm... I'm not sure whether anyone actually told you, but—"

She rolled her eyes. "I guessed a long time ago, Rory. Frankly, I'm surprised the others didn't, considering he isn't remotely like a regular owl."

"Except when it comes to dropping rodents down the sink." I frowned. "Hang on, I thought you were the one who cast the spell enabling him to speak in the first place."

She snorted. "That was an attempt to cover for him. One which he didn't appreciate, I might add."

"So he knew you were already aware of his secret." His reaction the other day was just for show, was it? I spun around, but Sylvester had already taken flight off the balcony. "That owl."

Cass's laughter sounded behind me while I marched downstairs in pursuit of the owl. I almost hoped he'd throw me into the Forbidden Room and give me the chance to interrogate him directly, but no such luck. I reached the ground floor without being challenged.

"Sylvester!" I raised my voice, but no response came.

"Rory?" Estelle called to me from the front desk. "You have a visitor."

I approached the desk and found a very confused Xavier waiting for me. "Rory, what's going on?"

"That owl," I snarled. "Turns out Cass knew his secret all along. She confirmed it. He threw me in the Forbidden Room the other day for no reason whatsoever."

"Typical," said Estelle. "He didn't try any more tricks on you, did he?"

"No, but there are some students hanging around outside the Artefacts Division. I think they want to use that room to practise their spells, but I'm not sure playing chicken with spikes will end well. Even rubber ones."

She grinned. "I can watch to make sure they don't get into anything else, but I think you've earned the chance to leave early. Right, Rory?"

I didn't argue with that. "Sure. I'll see you later."

Xavier and I left the library, hand in hand.

"Never a dull moment," he remarked. "How was the exam?"

"Not too bad," I replied. "Though I seem to have missed all the news. Did you hear—"

"George was jailed, yes," he said. "In the same prison he used to work at, but he won't stay for long. He didn't manage to actually capture the dragon, after all."

"No, but I doubt he'll stick around in Ivory Beach afterwards, considering the whole pack wants their hands on him."

Not to mention my Aunt Candace, who remained furious despite her refusal to admit to being duped. She refused to believe that George had simply been humouring her to find out the dragon's location and remained convinced that everything had been going fine until I'd interrupted her date. Or Evangeline. Regardless, she'd managed to get no fewer than three new book ideas out of the whole fiasco, which would keep her occupied.

"Hey, it's your friend." Xavier halted, seeing Robin and Tansy crossing the square nearby. "Robin."

"Oh, hi," I said to Robin. "Are you heading home?"

"Soon." She carried a rucksack over one shoulder and held a long shimmering stick in her hand. It resembled a large, ornate wand. *Is that the sceptre?* "I wanted to talk to you, but I heard you were taking an exam, so I decided to wait. How'd it go?"

"Good, for a wonder," I replied. "Your family didn't stay?"

"My mother and brother are already on their way out of town, but I wanted to come and say goodbye first."

"Does that mean they aren't bringing the covens or the local witch council with them?"

"Of course they aren't," she said. "We checked the rules. There's nothing your family is doing that goes against the laws, regardless of how unconventional that library of yours is. Not everything in the magical world can be contained within a clear set of guidelines. I should know that given that I got picked as Head Witch and not my mother."

My gaze went to the long, glowing stick in her hand. "Is that…?"

"Yeah, that's my ceremonial sceptre," she said. "And the reason I came here to the library—to find out why it picked me. I'm still not clear on that one, but I didn't expect to leave with a dragon. It's been an interesting trip."

"You're taking the baby dragon with you?"

"No, but we're helping the family relocate their nest elsewhere," she said. "Not what I expected from a holiday, but I'm glad I came here."

"So am I," I said, surprised to find that I meant it. "If just because if you didn't remove the dragon's nest to another location, all three of them would probably be living on the third floor of the library instead."

"Oh yeah, I can imagine," she said. "Anyway—gotta go. Good luck with everything."

"You too." I waved her off and then turned back to Xavier. "Wanna head to the Black Dog?"

"Definitely."

We veered towards the seafront, where the waves lapped against the shore. Not a single mystery monster was to be seen. After enjoying a nice meal at the pub, we made our leisurely way to the pier to watch the sunset over the waves. A breeze swept in off the coast, and movement in the corner of my eye clued me in to a vampire's stealthy approach.

Laney stepped into view. "Hey."

"Hey. Are you on your way to a lesson?"

"Yeah, but I figured you'd be out here," she answered. "I know you don't want Evangeline finding out your secrets, but I've got a plan."

Ah. We hadn't had time to discuss how to keep Evangeline from learning Sylvester's true identity, but it'd been impossible to keep recent events from our resident vampire. With the amount of time Laney spent in Evangeline's company, it seemed inevitable that she'd glean the truth.

"A plan?" I echoed. "What is it?"

"Every time she mentions anything to do with your family, I'm going to sing in my head as loudly as possible to annoy her," she said. "I know it sounds ridiculous, but I've been doing the same whenever she starts poking around asking about your dad's journal."

"You have?"

"Yes, and it worked." She grinned. "I know you don't believe she's that easily annoyed, but there's nothing that irritates her more than the sound of someone singing peppy music when she's trying to poke into their thoughts."

A smile tugged at my mouth despite myself. "Be careful, though."

"I will. Are you heading back to the library now?"

"Sure." I glanced at Xavier, who smiled back at me. "Why?"

"You should know the others have all turned in early, and even Sylvester isn't hanging around. If I were you, I'd seize the day. Or night." She shot me a wink. "Have fun, you two."

And then she was gone in a blink of the eye while my face flushed up to my hairline. "Erm... right."

"Interesting," Xavier remarked dryly. "Should we head back?"

"Yeah." Despite the cool night air, heat burned my neck and face. "Singing to annoy Evangeline. Never thought that would work."

"I don't know, it sounds like an effective way of keeping someone out of your thoughts," he commented. "Did you ever find out why Evangeline met with the chief of the werewolf pack, by the way?"

"If I had to guess, Evangeline probably picked up on George's treachery. It wasn't all about my aunt's odd taste in romantic partners after all."

He laughed under his breath. "I thought not."

We walked the rest of the way back to the library in silence, and tension sizzled in the air when Xavier turned to me as we reached the steps leading to the front door.

"When she said nobody was around," he said, "was she implying that nobody would disturb us if I came into the library with you?"

"Yes." My heartbeat fluttered in my fingertips. "Ah—I got Estelle to teach me a locking charm for my door, which I think will hold up even against a certain owl who likes to barge into my room in the night. It's up to you, though. Spending a night in a magical library isn't for the faint of heart."

He laughed. "You've really thought hard about this."

"I guess I have," I said sheepishly. "I really like you. I also like my family, but there are some things I want them to stay out of, and even the all-powerful embodiment of the library doesn't have to know everything."

"I have to agree." He smiled and kissed me lightly on the lips. "Relax, Rory. I'm with you every step of the way. Want to go in?"

"Sure." Taking his hand in mine, I pushed open the door, and we walked into the library.

ABOUT THE AUTHOR

Elle Adams lives in the middle of England, where she spends most of her time reading an ever-growing mountain of books, planning her next adventure, or writing. Elle's books are humorous mysteries with a paranormal twist, packed with magical mayhem.

She also writes urban and contemporary fantasy novels as Emma L. Adams.

Visit http://www.elleadamsauthor.com/ to find out more about Elle's books.